WILL SHAKESPEARE
AND THE
PIRATE'S FIRE

ROBERT J HARRIS

HarperCollins *Children's Books*

Many thanks to my wife Debby for all her help with this book and for everything else as well; my friend Jane Yolen for making me a writer; my agent Elizabeth Harding for all her support and encouragement; and to my editor Stella Paskins for her unfailing good nature.

First published in Great Britain by HarperCollins Children's Books 2006
HarperCollins *Children's Books* is an imprint of HarperCollins *Publishers* Ltd
77-85 Fulham Palace Road, Hammersmith, London, W6 8JB

www.harpercollinschildrensbooks.co.uk

1

Copyright © Robert J Harris 2006

ISBN 13: 978 0 00 719424 7
ISBN 10: 0 00 719424 2

Robert J Harris asserts the moral right to be identified as the author of the work.

Printed and bound in Great Britain by
Clays Ltd, St Ives plc

For Jill, who told me many years ago I was going to write this book.

THE PERSONS OF THE STORY

WILL SHAKESPEARE, *a young man of Stratford*

JOHN SHAKESPEARE, *father to Will*

MARY SHAKESPEARE, *mother to Will*

HAMNET SADLER, *friend to Will*

SIR THOMAS LUCY, *squire of Charlecote*

HENRY BEESTON
KIT BEESTON
TOM CRADDOCK
RALPH
\- *players*

KEMP, *a clown*

DR. JOHN DEE, *a scholar, or conjuror*

CALEB, *his assistant*

MAGDALENA, *an airy spirit*

WALTER RALEIGH, *an adventurer*

SIR FRANCIS WALSINGHAM, *secretary of state to the Queen*

CHARLES SLEDD, *an inquisitor*

BERNARDINO DE MENDOZA, *the Spanish ambassador*

DUKE OF ANJOU, *a French lord*

LOK, *a boatman*

THOMASINA, *attendant to the Queen*

BELLOWS & DULWORTH, *constables*

DONAL, *a pirate*

ELIZABETH, *Queen of England*

Soldiers, Pirates, Townsfolk, &c.

I

The Hunters Hunted

"I'd give a lot for a good horse right now," panted Will Shakespeare, leaning heavily against the trunk of a looming oak tree. He wiped some sweat from his brow with the cuff of his jerkin and sucked in the sharp February air.

They had been running so hard his friend Hamnet could hardly summon the breath to speak. "I'd settle for a hole in the ground," he gasped, "and some branches to cover ourselves with."

"Look how they're beating the bushes," Will pointed out. "It'll take more than a few twigs to save us."

Hamnet poked his head out for a peek. Will caught the

back of his jerkin and yanked him down. "Stay down, you clodpole! They'll see you!"

"You wouldn't think they'd be so stirred up over a few rabbits," sighed Hamnet. "Maybe we should have just picked some berries and gone home."

Hamnet Sadler was only a few months younger than Will and they had been friends for the entire fourteen years they had been growing up in Stratford. They had taken more than a few chances together, but if they were convicted of poaching a public whipping was the lightest sentence they could expect.

They both hugged the tree's shadow as they spied on Sir Thomas Lucy's men. There were a dozen of them, poking in the bushes with hunting spears, determined to flush out the young poachers. They were a tough, hard crew, the sort who could be depended on to carry out any order, no matter how cruel, as long as they were paid for the deed.

The squire himself perched uneasily astride his fat, grey gelding. He surveyed the ground and yapped out his orders. "There, Cobb, there!" he shrilled. "I swear by God I saw something move among those brambles."

"Just a bird, sir!" Cobb called back.

Will sank back into the shadows. "That nag of his couldn't outrun Widow Tanner's donkey," he said.

"It's his men will outrun us if he spots us," said Hamnet. "And they're a mean lot."

Will bit his lower lip and looked around. This was a wild, tangled country, too dense and thorny for deer – nothing for a proper nobleman to brag about – but Sir Thomas guarded it like it was the Garden of Eden. Charlecote Warren the locals called it, for it was rich in rabbits, hare and game birds.

Will fingered the bow that hung at his side, thinking of the pair of rabbits and the fat guinea fowl he had bagged. Hamnet had only got a stringy-looking hare, but he was well content with his prize. England's longbowmen had once made her armies invincible, but in these days of gunpowder the bow had become a poacher's weapon.

Hamnet shook his head like an old man. "I wish you'd stop getting us into fixes like this, Will. It was bad enough when we were just filching apples."

"Life will be quiet enough when you're in the grave," said Will, giving his friend an encouraging thump on the arm. "Besides, somebody has to goad Old Lousy."

"Come on, use your eyes!" Sir Thomas Lucy was telling his men. "They can't have disappeared like vapour!"

"I think I recognised one of them, sir," said one of the hunters. "John Shakespeare's boy."

"Shakespeare!" Lucy pronounced the name as a hateful

hiss. "That insolent brogger! He's been more trouble to me than floods and plague. But if I take his boy up on a poaching charge, that will knock the mischief out of him."

"Will, they know who you are!" Hamnet exclaimed through gritted teeth.

"He's just guessing," said Will. "They weren't close enough to see our faces. If we can get back to Stratford ahead of them, they won't be able to prove a thing."

"And how are we going to do that?" Hamnet asked. "Are you going to conjure up a griffin to carry us on its back?"

"No need for magic," Will answered. "If we crawl on our bellies through the gorse there, we can make it to the stream without being spotted. Then we can wade through the water till we're clear of Charlecote."

"So we're to be drowned, dirty… and… and…" Hamnet faltered over a final word.

"Desperate," Will finished for him.

"That's not what I was trying to say," Hamnet complained.

"Come on," urged Will, pulling his friend into the undergrowth beside him. "Desperate men can't hang around waiting on luck to save their hide."

Wriggling along on their hands and knees, they pressed through the rough bushes. Again and again they became snagged on thorns and had to carefully ease themselves loose without giving away their position.

All at once the drumming of hooves made them stop dead and press their faces to the earth. The hoof beats came closer and the shadow of a mounted figure passed over them. Hamnet squeezed his eyes tight shut in an effort to ignore the danger, but Will glanced up to see sir Thomas reining in only a few yards away. He could smell the horse's acrid sweat and hear the breath puffing in its nostrils.

The squire stood up in the stirrups and peered off to the south and west. "Are you sure they came this way? I'll not be made to look a fool."

"They came this way as sure as there's apples," answered his man Cobb. "That's not to say they ain't sneaked past us like adders in the grass."

"What's that?" cried a voice.

"Where?" Sir Thomas demanded. "Where?"

"I saw something move, sir! Over there by the rocks!"

Will froze like a statue, but Sir Thomas was not looking in their direction. He spurred his horse into a lumbering canter, waving his men forward.

"Here's our chance," said Will, giving Hamnet a sharp nudge. They crawled on their bellies to the bank of the stream, then slid over the edge and into the shallow water.

"Oh, it's cold enough to freeze your cullions off!" Hamnet moaned.

Will shivered. "It's only till we get well out of sight, Hamnet. Stay down now!"

Crouching so low it made their backs ache, they sloshed along slowly, careful not to attract attention. They had only gone a short way when Hamnet slipped and plunged completely under the water. Will grabbed him under the arms and hauled him up, dripping and coughing.

"Hush!" Will warned.

They stood as still as stone, listening for some cry of alarm. Leaning on Hamnet's shoulder, Will pushed himself up on tiptoes to scout around. "It's all right," he said. "They're going the other way."

Hamnet picked some dank weeds out of his hair and coughed again. "I think I've swallowed a minnow, Will."

"Don't worry, they're not poisonous."

"But I can feel it wriggling inside me."

"That's just your breakfast coming back on you. Forget about it. Come on."

Will started forward then realised Hamnet wasn't following. Turning round, he saw his friend had turned dreadfully pale.

"I'm going to heave, Will," choked Hamnet. "There's no help for it."

Will backed away so quickly he almost toppled over himself. Hamnet doubled over and threw up with a noise like a drain emptying. He finished with a final cough and straightened up.

"Are you fit to go on now?" Will asked.

Hamnet nodded and forced a wan smile.

"Here, I'll give you a hand," said Will, taking his friend by the arm. As they waded onwards he muttered, "And I'll remember not to fish here for a while."

At the point where the stream flowed into the River Avon, the boys climbed up on to higher ground and headed south. It was a chilly day, and their sodden clothes clung to them like ice. Clopton Bridge, leading into Stratford, was as welcome a sight as a warm fire and a haunch of mutton. In summer children splashed about under its arches and boys waded about in search of trout and pike. It was too cold for that now and the otters had the run of the fishing to themselves.

Further downriver, the spire of Holy Trinity poked at the sky. The centre of the parish, the church was not the comforting symbol it once had been. Many had fallen foul of the law because of their refusal to attend the new services decreed by the government, Will's own father amongst them.

Marching briskly up Bridge Street into town, the boys were startled by a sudden uproar of voices off to their left. "An ambush!" Hamnet cried, gripping Will by the arm. Will laughed and shook himself loose. It was only a raucous sing-song starting off inside the Peacock Tavern. Weak-kneed with relief, they carried on up the road to the market cross.

"We'll split up here," said Will. "Nobody knows you were with me, so there's no sense you catching any trouble."

"I'll take my share if it will help you, Will," said Hamnet, shuffling his feet on the cobbles.

Will put a grateful hand on his friend's shoulder and smiled. "I know you would, Hamnet. But for now, the best thing for us both is to lie low for a few days."

"Will, look!" Hamnet exclaimed suddenly. He was pointing back they way they had come.

Will turned quickly and saw to his horror the mounted figure of Old Lousy crossing Clopton Bridge, with his minions filing along behind him.

2

Lord Strange's Men

"Go!" said Will, giving Hamnet a firm shove.

Hamnet nodded and darted off down the High Street to the Sadler family home. Will dashed up Henley Street to his father's house. Like the other houses on the street it had a frame of sturdy oak timbers filled in with walls of clay and mortar, the latticed windows shut tight against the cold.

The winter of 1578 had been grievously hard, especially for the Shakespeares, whose daughter Anne had died of a chill aged only five. The new year still hadn't wriggled loose of winter's grasp and Mary Shakespeare fretted anxiously over the rest of her children every time they set foot outdoors. Will knew she wouldn't be pleased to find him soaked to the skin and caked with muck. As the eldest, he was expected to set an example for Gilbert, Joan and little Richard.

Opening the door as quietly as he could, he crept up the hallway, hoping he'd be able to clean up before—

"Will? Is that you?"

It was his mother's voice, coming from the kitchen dead ahead. Before he could twitch a muscle, the door opened and Mary Shakespeare strode out, dusting flour from her hands as she came. She pulled up with a start and stared.

"Will! You look like somebody's used you to plough up a field!"

"I fell," Will said lamely.

His mother took a firm hold of his collar and steered him through the left-hand doorway. This was John Shakespeare's workroom and he was bent over his table, cutting out a glove-shaped pattern from a stretch of soft kidskin.

There were oak rafters overhead, a brick fireplace and a floor that was a patchwork of broken stones, fitted together like the pieces of a puzzle. Animal hides in various states of preparation hung from the walls alongside a variety of blades for cutting them to shape. The far wall was covered by a painted hanging showing their local hero, Guy of Warwick, slaying the monstrous Wild Dun Cow. The cow had been a fairy beast that provided the whole county with milk, until a witch milked it dry and turned it into a man-eater. It was John Shakespeare's favourite story.

As his wife and son entered, John looked up from his work and set aside his curved, razor-sharp knife. "What's the bother?" he asked.

"You tell me!" answered his wife. "You said he was out running an errand for you."

"Did I?" John Shakespeare hooked his thumbs into his leather belt and did his best to glower at his son. "Well, what have you been up to, Will?"

Will understood that this was one of those times when the best course was to tell the truth. "I was over in Charlecote Park, hunting for rabbits."

His father sighed. "I took you out of school to help me at my work, not to poach off Charlecote land."

"I thought I'd do us more good by bringing some food into the house instead of stitting around sewing up leather," said Will. "I'm no good at that work anyway."

John Shakespeare scowled a moment, giving his wife a sidelong glance to check that she approved of his stern demeanour. Then he leaned towards his son and asked in a conspirator's whisper. "Did you catch anything?"

"That's not the point, John!" Mary Shakespeare protested.

Will grinned and laid his bag down on the table. He yanked it open to proudly display the contents to his father. John Shakespeare raised his eyebrows appreciatively and poked the fat rabbits with his forefinger.

"Well, I'll say this and not be denied: you're a better poacher than you are a glover."

"Maybe not," Will said hesitantly. "We nearly got caught... and one of Sir Thomas' men spotted me."

Mary Shakespeare gave a start of alarm, but her husband raised a hand to calm her. "How good a look did he get?" he asked Will.

"Not good, but I heard him say the name Shakespeare."

John Shakespeare rubbed his chin and pursed his lips, a sure sign that his shrewd brain was hard at work. "At a distance, on a grey day like this – we can deny it, make out you were elsewhere. Given time I can call in a few friendly witnesses."

Right then a fist pounded at the front door and a voice bellowed, "John Shakespeare! Open up there!"

Will's heart leapt in panic. "It's them!" he gasped. "I'm caught!"

"Oh, look at the state of you!" fretted his mother, touching a finger to Will's damp, dirty jerkin. "We can't pretend you've been home all day."

"Steady yourselves," said John Shakespeare in a commanding tone. "I've a few tricks in hand yet. Mary, you answer the door, but take your time opening it. Fiddle the latch like it's stuck. If they ask about Will, say he's off in Wilmcote with your Arden relatives. Been there a day and a half."

"John, you're making a liar of me!" Mary accused. "Again!"

"You've such a pretty a tongue for lying I hate to see it wasted," said John, giving her a quick kiss on the cheek. He took Will's bow and arrows and stashed them under the table with the bag of game. "Come on, Will, it's out the back way for us. We'll give them the dodge!"

Will couldn't help but smile. His father was the fiercest schemer in all of Warwickshire, and even now, with his fortunes at their lowest and troubles on every side, his wits still leapt to a challenge, like Guy of Warwick drawing his sword on a dragon.

"John Shakespeare!" bellowed the voice again. There was more beating at the door, louder this time.

"I'm coming, I'm coming!" Mary Shakespeare called,

moving down the hallway in tiny steps. "Give me a moment to make myself decent!"

Father and son bolted through the kitchen and out of the back door into the yard. There were two outbuildings here where John Shakespeare stored the supplies he needed for his leather business, as well as other items he traded in on the side, like wool and grain. Dodging behind one of these, they made sure the coast was clear before slipping out the back gate.

Looking as casual as possible, so as not to draw attention from passers-by, they made their way through the empty cattle market, back towards the town centre.

"Where are we going?" Will asked.

John Shakespeare pointed towards the spire of the Guild Chapel. "Just there, boy."

"The Guild Hall?" said Will, puzzled. "But why?"

"Have you forgotten? Henry Beeston and his lads are in town," replied his father. "You know – Lord Strange's Men."

"The players you mean?" said Will.

"I did a favour or two for old Beeston when I had charge of public entertainments," said his father. "He's just the man to help us out."

Will knew that whenever players were in town they put on their show in the Guild Hall. Back when his father was the leading man on the council, they had front row seats for every performance. He remembered being taken along and delighting in the clowning, swordfights and dances which enlivened the plays.

But that was some years past, before the wool market collapsed, before men suffered financial punishments for not falling into line with the government's religion. John Shakespeare had been forced to sell off much of his property and incurred heavy debts in order to sustain his business. Yet still the prospect of a brighter future kept the sparkle in his eye.

"Will," he would tell his son, "one day we'll be the ones living in a manor house with our own coat of arms over the door, and the likes of Lousy Thomas Lucy will come begging to sit at our table."

"If we're going to have a coat of arms," Will would reply, "you need to make your mind up about how *Shakespeare* is supposed to be spelled."

They walked briskly down Ely Street then turned sharp right up Chapel Street until they came to the Guild Hall and its adjoining chapel. Will knew the building well. The school he had attended from the ages of seven to twelve was located on the upper floor.

When his father had taken him out of school to help with

his ailing glove-making business Will had been both happy and sad. Most of the lessons were as dull as mud, but he had loved the stories they read. Some were in English, some in Latin – and there were poems, comedies and histories, tales of faraway places and long ago.

"This way, Will," said John Shakespeare, leading his son away from the front entrance. "We're not here for the show."

Slipping unnoticed through a side door, they made their way down a wood-panelled passage, only to find their path blocked by a stout man carrying a stick.

"Out you go!" he boomed. "We'll have no spectators backstage and no free peeks at the show!"

He placed a hand on John Shakespeare's chest and started to push him back. Will's father immediately planted his feet and gave the man a hefty shove that almost toppled him over. He thrust out his chin and jabbed an angry finger in the air.

"I've no time for your fiddle-faddle," he intoned. "I'm here on behalf of the Queen's Commission to report any hints of treason or immorality. If you don't step aside, I'll have you in the stocks before you can cough!"

Will's father had held many prominent positions in Stratford, from ale-taster to bailiff, and he could assume the manner of a belligerent official as easily as putting on a hat.

The stout man hastily swept off his cap and made a humble bow. "A thousand apologies, your honour," he said. "Nobody told me there was to be an inspection."

"Only your ignorance makes me lenient," said John Shakespeare, sweeping grandly past him. As they entered the great hall he turned to Will and said with a chuckle, "These fellows aren't the only actors around here."

With that they passed through the door into a different world.

3

The King Must Die

A curtain had been hung across one end of the Guild Hall, giving the players a private place screened off from the audience. The whole area was filled with bustle as costumes were tossed about, props exchanged and scripts passed from hand to hand.

A boy's voice singing some sort of hymn filtered through the curtain and a moment later the boy himself came offstage, lifting his skirts as he traipsed down the small wooden steps. He was dressed as an oriental queen.

Women were forbidden by law to appear on the stage, so female roles were played by clean-shaven young men. The boy was accompanied by two older men dressed as murderous ruffians with daggers in their hands.

"Don't handle me so rough out there," the player queen complained peevishly. "You're creasing me royal robes." He pulled off his crown and the long black wig that was pinned to it, then rubbed a hand over the short-cropped hair beneath.

One of the ruffians poked him with the butt end of his dagger and laughed. "It's Cruel and Murder we're playing, Tom, not Kind and Coddling."

A young man in the colourful patchwork costume of a clown was bounding up the steps. "Spice it up out there, Kemp!" one of the others encouraged him as he disappeared through the curtain. His appearance on stage brought a cheer of recognition from the crowd.

There were seven or eight people backstage now, but they were milling around so busily they seemed like twice that number. Piled all about were boxes of fabric, boxes of wigs, pots of paint and flasks of powder. John Shakespeare bobbed this way and that, trying to see past them. Only slightly muffled by the curtain, Will could hear the clown declaiming on the stage:

"Cambyses put a judge to death – that was a good deed –
But to kill the young child was worse to proceed,
To murder his brother, and then his own wife –
So help me God and holydom, it is pity of his life!"

At the far side of all the backstage bustle stood a regal figure with long white hair and a bushy beard, a painted plaster crown perched on his head. He was mouthing words off a script in his hand while a boy fastened a belt round his midriff. Sticking out from this belt was the hilt and half the blade of a wooden sword daubed with red paint.

"There's the man," said John Shakespeare, elbowing his way through the other actors.

The boy pulled down the makeshift king's robe so that the fake sword poked out through a convenient rent in the purple cloth then stood back, regarding his work with satisfaction. "You're properly done to death there, dad," he said.

"Harry!" said Will's father, offering his hand. "Harry Beeston!"

Beeston looked up from his script with a smile of recognition. "John Shakespeare!" he said, giving a vigorous handshake. "I heard you had – shall we say – *retired* from public life."

"You know what it is to have creditors hounding your tracks, Harry."

"I do indeed," said Beeston, setting aside his script and making sure his crown was sitting straight. "You've come a bit late to catch my *Cambyses*, John. Show's nearly done and we're off in the morning."

"I didn't come for the play," Will's father began.

"No time to chat, John," Beeston interrupted. "About to go on stage and die."

John Shakespeare put a restraining hand on Beeston's arm as he made to go. "Cling to life a little longer, if you please, Harry," he said. "My boy Will here's in a spot of trouble, and you owe me a favour, if you recall."

Beeston tapped his head with his forefinger. "I keep an exact ledger of every kindness right here, be sure of that. What's the pickle?"

John Shakespeare leaned close so that only Beeston could hear him. "Sir Thomas Lucy's after him for poaching."

"Lucy?" Beeston bristled at the name. "The villain that tried to ban our show? Claimed it was lewd – and seditious to boot?"

"The very same, Harry."

"Then the favour's yours, John. We'll hoodwink that pompous poltroon."

One of the other players, who was peering round the edge of the curtain, turned and said, "There's some trouble out there, Harry. A bunch of louts forcing their way through the crowd."

John Shakespeare took a look for himself and ground his teeth. "It's Lousy Lucy and his men," he said. "No time to waste, Harry."

Beeston tapped the boy who had been dressing him on the shoulder and pointed at Will. "Kit, trick him up in a wench's garb. Quick change now!"

"I'm not dressing up as a girl!" Will protested, raising his hands to keep Kit at bay.

"Do as he says, Will!" said John Shakespeare sharply. "You stay with Harry and his crew until I tell you otherwise. I'll get out front and stall Lucy and his boys." He slipped around the curtain and out of sight.

Will's shoulders slumped and he let Kit pull an outsized crimson dress over his head, yanking it down to cover his filthy clothes. The boy tutted as he struggled to straighten out the folds on the ill-fitting gown. "We're going to have to wash this as soon as it's off."

"Briskly, Kit, briskly!" Beeston urged. "Must get him on stage before the squire's men start poking around back here."

"On stage!" exclaimed Will in shock, as Kit planted a russet wig on his head. "Dressed like this?"

Beeston tapped himself on the nose and winked. "A man can't see what's right under his nose, not unless his eyes fall out." He whipped out a kerchief and wiped the worst of the dirt from Will's face. "A spot of red there, Kit, that should set the whole thing off."

Kit brushed the trailing locks of the wig aside and dabbed red make-up on to Will's cheeks. "There!" he said. "Your own mum would hardly know you now."

"She wouldn't want to," said Will glumly.

"Right, up you go!" said Beeston, propelling him towards the stage steps.

Out front Kemp the clown was uttering his climactic lines to introduce the king:

"He has shed so much blood that his will be shed.
If it come to pass, in faith, then his will be sped."

"But what am I supposed to do?" Will protested. "I'm no actor."

"Stand in the background and look pretty," said Beeston, "or stupid. Makes no difference. When I make my entrance, look appalled if you will, shed a tear even. There'll be few enough of those for old Cambyses."

Irritably, Kemp repeated the king's cue, louder this time:

"If it come to pass, in faith, then he is sped!"

Will tried to resist but Beeston and Kit pushed him up the stairway and through the curtains. He stumbled out on to the stage, almost tripping over the hem of his overlong dress. The crowd gave a roar of laughter at his clumsiness and he looked up to find himself confronted by a sea of expectant faces.

Some of them murmured and pointed, wondering who the newcomer was supposed to be. "That's not King Cambyses!" somebody called out. "Looks more like my sister Kate!" yelled another.

Will glanced to his left and saw Sir Thomas Lucy and his men force their way through the side curtain into the backstage area. Will's father was in the midst of them, firmly held between two of the squire's minions. None of them were looking at the stage.

"It's as I told you," Will could hear his father saying, "I came here alone to pay a visit to my old friend Henry Beeston. My boy's been gone at least a day."

Kemp the clown was as surprised as the audience to see

Will emerge. He fiddled with the tassels on his patchwork costume as he recovered his composure then struck a confident pose and gestured towards Will, saying,

"Ah yes, you wonder, good people, who might this be,
A mysterious maid, but she is known to me…"

He waved his hand vaguely, as if trying to conjure up more words out of the air.

"Though strangely changed by death she surely has been,
I swear this is the spirit of the lately murdered queen."

A great "Ooh!" went up from the crowd at this revelation and many of them made pitying noises over the queen's awful fate.

Before Will could decide what to do, the curtain fluttered behind him and Beeston came barging past. A chorus of boos and jeers greeted the king as he staggered to the front of the stage. The fake sword was sticking out of his side and he clutched it tight with his right hand. Looking up to the heavens, he gave a deep groan that resonated throughout the hall.

"Out! Alas!" he moaned. *"What shall I do? My life is*

finished! Wounded I am by sudden chance; my blood is minished."

"Good riddance to you!" bawled a stout woman at the back of the hall, sparking an uproar of agreement.

"*As I on horseback up did leap,*" groaned King Cambyses, his voice hoarse with pain. "*My sword from scabbard shot, and ran me thus into the side – as you right well may see.*"

He displayed his bloody wound to the crowd who let out an enormous cheer, then he slumped to the floor and continued his dying speech. Kemp stood over him pulling faces, but warily, as if the king were a wounded beast that might still turn on him.

Some of Lucy's men came out front and started pressing through the crowd, searching for their fugitive. Sir Thomas himself reappeared, John Shakespeare close behind. Will's father was doing his best to distract the squire by talking about the bad winter, the price of bread and anything else he could think of.

Finally King Cambyses breathed his last and Kemp leaned over him with his hands on his hips. "*Alas, good king!*" he said sadly. "*Alas, he is gone!*" He allowed himself a long pause then added loudly, "*The devil take me if for him I make any moan!*"

The crowd roared their approval.

Will hoped fervently that the play was done, and that he could vanish behind the curtain once more. But Kemp was still speaking, and worse – Sir Thomas Lucy had turned to stare directly at the stage.

4

A Handful of Luck

Will flinched, as if the squire's eyes were a pair of musket balls about to be fired at him. He toyed with his wig, tugging the russet locks in front of his face.

Just as he was thinking of making a run for it, Kemp launched himself into a mad dance. He capered round the royal corpse like a prisoner set free of the gallows. He hopped this way and that, twirled left, then right, then leapt over the dead king to land precariously on the very edge of the stage. He tottered there, his arms windmilling frantically as he tried to keep balance.

The crowd roared and clapped, and Will saw that even

Lousy Lucy was laughing and applauding the clown's acrobatics. Kemp drew out his predicament a little longer then flung himself into a back somersault that carried him right over the dead king to land on his feet with a flourish.

The hall was rocked by whistles, guffaws and cheers. Three lords marched solemnly on to the stage and lifted the king up. As they carried him away, Kemp hooked his arm through Will's and hauled him off through the curtains.

"Where the duck eggs did you churn up from?" he asked.

"I think you mean 'turn up'," said Will. He couldn't help but smile. He felt as if the continuing applause was not only for the play, but his own narrow escape as well.

"If I meant to call you a turnip I would have said so," the clown informed him haughtily as they reached the bottom of the steps.

The king had come back to furious life and stood fuming indignantly at the clown. "Kemp!" he said. "How many times have I told you to keep within the bounds of the script?"

"More times than I can count," Kemp answered him. "But it's hardly my fault if you see fit to introduce a ghost into the play, or whatever this new boy of yours is supposed to be."

"Dad," said Kit, tugging at Beeston's sleeve, "your bows."

"Well recollected, Kit," said the king, his bad humour melting away. He bounded up the steps as quickly as a man half his age and presented himself on stage to wild applause.

"I must go take my bows also," said Kemp to Will. "But I advise you to stay congealed back here, Mistress Spirit."

"I'll keep out of sight," Will assured him. "I'll be *indivisible*."

The clown laughed to hear his own word plays turned about on him, then raced up on to the stage with the other actors to accept the enthusiastic cheers of the crowd.

The early morning air was so cold their breath hung in misty clouds before their faces. Lord Strange's Men had risen with the dawn for, as Henry Beeston told Will, "We want to be long gone before that simple-minded squire notices that he might have been tricked."

After a hasty breakfast they had loaded all their costumes, props and other baggage on to two horse drawn wagons and set out on the north-bound road towards Warwick. Will was reclining at the back of the lead wagon beside Kit Beeston.

Henry Beeston was seated beside the driver, his nose deep in a thick script. Also in the wagon were young Tom Craddock, who had played Cambyses' queen, and Ralph, a burly fellow who had been one of the queen's murderers.

"Ferdinando Stanley, Lord Strange, is our patron," Kit was explaining. "He lives many miles away in Derby, but his name stands as surety of our honesty and good behaviour."

"But why should he lend you his name if he never even comes with you?" Will asked.

"Lord Strange's Men were in origin entertainers to the Stanley family," Kit replied, "and when we took our act out into the country at large, Lord Strange continued his patronage. Other nobles have their own companies, the Earl of Leicester for one – and he's the Queen's favourite. The Queen's ministers have forbidden players to perform unless they have the patronage of some nobleman or other."

All of a sudden the horses were reined in and the wagon stopped with a jolt that nearly threw Kit out the back.

"What's this?" Kit wondered. "Surely there can't be robbers this close to Stratford?"

Will craned around for a look and saw to his surprise that it was his father who had caused the halt. John Shakespeare walked up to the wagon and shook hands with Beeston. The two men drew their heads in close and exchanged a few words.

Will jumped off the back of the wagon and ran to his father. "Are you here to take me home?" he asked.

"Things are a mite hot for that yet," said John Shakespeare.

He took his son aside and laid a hand on his shoulder. "You know Lucy's been hounding me for a long time now, looking for some excuse to cast me in gaol. Unlucky for him, I've a lot of friends in these parts ready to stand up for me."

"Maybe you should just go to church and say the prayers they tell you to," said Will. "Life would be easier then."

His father's face clouded into a frown. "You know my loyalties, Will. I grew up with the Roman way and I'll not cast it off like a craven tossing away his sword to flee the field of battle. But it's a canny game I have to play and you'd best keep out of it for a while."

"For how long?" Will asked anxiously.

"A month or two, maybe more," his father answered. "Until all this blows over and Lousy Lucy finds somebody else to vent his spite on. I tried to give Harry some money for your upkeep, but he'd have none of it. Said you'll be working for your keep."

Will pulled a face. "No more acting, I hope! Being made a fool of once is enough."

John Shakespeare hefted the leather bag he was carrying at his side. "I've brought you a few comforts. There's some clothes and some of your mother's best cakes inside. And there's this too."

He loosened the cord that fastened the neck of the bag and pulled out a book. "Your mother wanted you to have it," he said, handing the book to his son. "She bought it in the market at Coventry and was keeping it for your birthday, but now…"

Will opened the book and ran his fingers gently down the page like he was testing the softness of silk. "It's Goldsmith's translation of Ovid's *Metamorphoses*," he breathed. This was the book he had loved best at school.

"That's a jawcracker," said John Shakespeare. "What's it about?"

"Gods and monsters," said Will with a gleam in his eye. "The Flood and the fall of Troy."

"Heroes too, I hope," said his father. "And speaking of heroes, I've brought you a gift of my own."

Will closed the book and looked up expectantly. His father spread an empty hand before him. Will stared hard, but all he could see were the lines on his bare palm.

"What is it?"

"Why, it's good luck, Will, ripe as a blueberry and ready for plucking. But you must be quick to catch it. Go on!"

Will knew this game well, for they had played it many

times before. John Shakespeare would offer his son some raisins or dates in the flat of his hand, but Will had to snatch them before his father closed his fist.

Will licked his lips, met his father's gleeful gaze – then grabbed quick as a blink. Has father whipped his hand away and each of them held his fist tight shut in front of his face.

"Let's see then," said John Shakespeare, slowly uncurling his fingers. His eyebrows arched up and a slow whistle slipped though his lips.

"You've whisked most of it away, and that's for sure," he said. "But you've left a wee bit to see me through. I'd best keep it safe until its needed," he added, putting his hand in his pocket.

Will opened his own hand and nodded approvingly. "That's the prettiest luck in all England," he said. "You couldn't buy better at the Queen's own court."

"What are you going to do with it?" asked his father.

Will stuffed his hand in his pocket to keep the luck safe. "Come back a few inches taller," he said, "and maybe a few pennies richer."

"Just make sure you come back with some stories to tell me," said John Shakespeare.

Caris Parentibus a filio suo amantissimo,

That is how they taught us to write letters at School. In Latin. "To my deare parents from their loving sonne" it says. Well, that's enough of that! Master Henry Beeston has granted me a sheete of his precious paper to write to you. I am glad of a change from copying out scripts for the Players. Ever since he learned how neatly I can write, Master Beeston has been employing me on such tasks until I sweare my pen fingers are benumbed.

I had thought to alter a word here and there, but Master Beeston took me strongly to task and warned me against such interference. "A word is a dangerous thing, Master Shaxpere," says he. "Misplace one word of the Bible and all Religion is o'erthrown; speake one hasty word to the wrathful mob and bloody rebellion is loosed." I think he protests too much. I only wanted some of the lines to sound better.

We have travelled far these past many weekes, to townes whose names I had not even heard. We set up our show in halls, courtyards and innes, and when there is no other sort of stage, the backs of the two wagons serve as such. I have played some small parts, though only twice more have

43

I suffered to be a girl. The parts of queens and suchlike noble ladies are played by Tom Craddock, while Master Beeston's son Kit acts the milkmaids and serving girls. They have forced upon me some lessons in walking with a woman's gait, though it is a skill I do not prize.

I have been learning other parts of the Player's Art also. Master Henry Beeston has been teaching me to talk very loudly, which he calls Declamation. Kemp has offered me lessons in dancing, but I fear I might injure myself if I accept his offer, so boisterous is his jigging.

Ralph has given me lessons in how to make a fine showe of a sword fight on the stage. One of our most popular showes is The Tale of Robin Hood, and how the crowd do cheere when Robin attacks the wicked Sheriff of Nottingham with a cry of "Have at you and God's curse on him that flees!"

Master Beeston, I have noted, takes every opportunity to visit shoppes and markets where he can purchase old bookes, and yet most of them he never takes time to read. I questioned him on this and he told me he is buying them for collectors all over the country who paye him well for this service.

He sayes that when King Henry the VIIIth abolished

the monasteries, the crown and the nobles took the monks' lands and belongings. Their libraries were sold off and bookes they had collected for centuries were scattered far and wide. These are most specially valuable.

There is one among them so strangely writ, to my eyes it might as well be Greek. When I asked Master Beeston about it he laughed most heartily and said, "That is no ordinary booke there, Master Shaxpere. That is bought for a Wyzard, Dr John Dee by name." He intends to deliver this booke and take payment for it on our way to London. I don't know if I want to meet a Wyzard or no, except that it would make a tale very worth the telling.

I hope you are all well in Stratford, that father's businesse prospers, and that Gilbert, Joan and Richard are all in good health. I trust God to keep you safe and I pray He may put an end to my troubles with Squire Lucy. I Will be back with you soone, I hope, for I have a Will to be so.

Your wandering and affectionate Sonne,
                                        Will Shaxpere.

5

Pilgrims in the Storm

A violent storm came roaring across the land, cuffing the trees this way and that like a gigantic bully. Bulging, black clouds wrestled each other across a sky lashed by whips of lightning, while the rain beat down in torrents, pounding the earth into mud. It was so dark it was as if someone had flung a shroud over the whole country, and Will had to peer intently to make out the words on the page before him. He was huddled up at the back of the wagon beside Kit Beeston, the book his mother had given him propped up on his knees. Henry Beeston sat opposite, silently mouthing a dramatic speech from one of his plays.

The wagon moved in fits and jerks as the horses dragged their hooves through the mud. Everyone cringed when a ferocious gust of wind threatened to rip the cover off the wagon and a flurry of rain rattled along the sides.

"It's lucky for us these things are built sturdy," Kit commented nervously. When there was no response he said, "Still reading that book, Will?"

Will nodded. "This bit is about Jupiter, the king of the gods, sending a flood to drown the world."

Kit made a pained face. "Sounds a bit close to home, that." He peeped over Will's shoulder, but couldn't make out a word in the gloom. "Let's hear it then," he urged.

Will picked out a passage he thought would impress and started to read:

"As soon as he between his hands the hanging clouds
> *had crushed,*
With rattling noise adown from heaven the rain full
> *sadly gushed.*
The floods at random where they list, through all the
> *fields did stray,*
Men, beasts, trees, and with their gods were Churches
> *washed away."*

As if to accompany Will's reading, a clap of thunder boomed out like the roll of a monstrous drum.

"Do you hear that, Dad?" Kit asked his father.

Beeston looked up with a start, as though jolted out of a sound sleep. "What? Oh yes, very fine, very fine. A most appropriate verse, Master Shakespeare. Though you might infuse your tone with a greater measure of drama."

The wagon shook under another peal of thunder.

"Is this some of Dr John Dee's magic, do you think?" asked Will. "You said we were getting close to his house at Mortlake."

Beeston laughed. "When I said he was a wizard, Will, I only meant that some ignorant folk have called him that on account of his arcane studies. In truth he is a scholar, a philosopher, and – luckily for me – an insatiable collector of rare books."

"He's court astrologer to Queen Elizabeth," Kit told Will, "and she thinks he can read the future."

"Yes, he set the date for the queen's coronation after consulting the stars to divine the most favourable day," his father agreed. "That's a far cry from magic."

"But I've heard you say he talks to spirits," Kit insisted. "Maybe he's upset some of them and caused this foul weather."

"Hush, Kit," said Beeston. "The man's eccentricities

should not be misinterpreted as sorcery, especially since we plan to spend the night at his house. We can lay this storm at Nature's feet and leave it there."

The wagon jolted to a halt then lurched to one side so sharply it almost tossed Will from his seat. He clapped the book shut and stuffed it away in his pack. "What's happened?" he asked.

"If this were a ship, I'd say we were sinking," said Kit.

Henry Beeston pulled a wide brimmed hat out of one of the costume boxes and planted it on his head. He climbed out of the back of the wagon with Will following curiously. Ralph had dismounted from the driver's seat to calm the horses, which were stamping and snorting. Will could see that the wheels on the left side had sunk into a soft patch of mud and the animals hadn't the strength to pull them loose.

Beeston surveyed their predicament from under the broad brim of his hat. He twisted some strands of beard around his finger and was about to speak when a cry of alarm interrupted him. Will looked round to see the second wagon shudder to a stop as it also tipped over to one side.

"Matthew," Beeston addressed the driver testily, "could you not see the bind we're in?"

Matthew spat at the muddy ground. "Who can see anything in this murk?"

Ralph bent down for a closer look at the problem. "We'll have to pull out some boards and use them to prop up the wheels before we can pull free," he said. "It's going to take a while."

"It's a fix," Beeston declared grimly. "The very devil of a fix." He peered into the darkness like a mariner trying to spot land. "We can't be more than a mile or two from Dee's place at Mortlake House. Tell you what, Ralph, you get the wagons unstuck while I go on ahead to arrange our quarters."

He strode back to the rear of the wagon and gathered the players about him. He struck a regal pose and issued his instructions like a king arraying his army. "Kit, you oversee the operation, and make sure the rain doesn't get into the baggage. Master Shakespeare, fetch down that chest of books and follow me."

Will hauled the box off the back of the wagon and grunted under the weight. "Do we have to bring these along?"

"It will make an excellent impression, Will, and that is all-important," said Beeston. He strode off, leaving Will to heave the box along after him.

As the rain buffeted them relentlessly, Will was sure they would be lost within the hour, but Beeston marched confidently on as if their way were lit by a beacon. Will felt like the king's fool following his mad master on some insane pilgrimage. He toiled on under the weight of the box, afraid he might lose sight of Beeston and be utterly lost in the storm.

He was glad when they paused to rest amid a thicket of maple trees. The interlacing boughs provided some shelter from the downpour. Will set the box down and sat on it, shaking droplets of rain from his hair.

"We're going to an awful lot of trouble to deliver some books," he huffed.

"Delivering the books isn't the half of it," said Beeston, leaning against one of the trees, "not even the quarter."

"What's the rest of it then?"

"Dr John Dee is more than just a customer of books, Will, he's a valuable contact at court. I've spent years leading my players from town to town, playing to the cheers of the commons. It's time we had the chance to play before the nobility – royalty even – that's where the real rewards lie."

"But you have your noble patron, Lord Strange," said Will.

"He's not a favourite of the Queen, unlike the Earl of Leicester. It's Leicester's Men that get the tasty jobs, like providing the royal revels, not poor old Henry Beeston and his boys."

"So how will Dr Dee help?"

"He has the Queen's ear, lad. If he were to drop a few compliments about Strange's Men, arrange for us to perform at the court, then we would be welcomed with open arms into the home of every noble in the land. And there's more. It would provide us with protection."

"Protection?" Will echoed, puzzled.

Beeston nodded solemnly. "We players have our enemies, those who would ban our plays because they consider them immoral, obscene even. Some think we even stir the common folk to thoughts of rebellion. Yes, these are dangerous times, Will, when a word in the wrong place can send a man to the gallows."

Will coughed, feeling a sudden constriction in his throat. He thought he'd escaped a whipping by running off with the players. Could it be he'd let himself in for an even worse danger? He felt his breeches squelch as he shifted his rear upon the chest. "No time to tarry!" Beeston declared, stirring from his reverie. "Onward!"

Will rose wearily to his feet and picked up the chest. Abandoning their shelter, the pair trudged out once more into the howling storm. After what felt like miles of trekking through the rain and mire Beeston finally pulled up short. He spread out his hands dramatically before him, as if there was a whole crowd of people there to witness his performance instead of one bedraggled boy.

"There it is, Will," he announced, "Mortlake House!"

6

The House of Doctor Dee

Will stared ahead but could see only a vague black bulk set against the rain-drenched gloom. Then a bolt of lightning cracked the sky and in the flash Will saw the whole house.

It was a vast, rambling structure. The central, stone-built bastion reared up five storeys high, the upper floors piled crazily on top of each other like badly balanced bricks. Adjoining wings jutted out on both sides, their roofs capped with mismatched gables and turrets. At ground level, further extensions sprawled out this way and that like the roots of some enormous tree. Will had never seen anything so bizarre.

And then it was gone, swallowed up in the darkness of the storm. Will rubbed his eyes. It was as if he had caught a glimpse of some grotesque goblin palace.

"Ah, Will, what an entrance we'll make!" Beeston exclaimed. "Like two shipwrecked mariners emerging from a tempest!"

The possibility of shelter, a warm fire, perhaps even a hot meal, renewed Will's strength as he and Beeston hurried through the ill-tended grounds towards the great house. Yellow lights glimmered at one or two of the upper windows, but other than that the house was as dark as the surrounding landscape.

There was a brass knocker on the door in the shape of a crescent moon. Beeston gave two loud raps then stood back, his eyes raised to the floors above. When there was no response, he rapped again – louder this time – but still with no result.

"Maybe they can't hear us over the wind and the rain," Will suggested. "I suppose we could just wait here for the others to arrive."

"What? Stand here shivering for an hour or more?" Beeston exclaimed. "What sort of an entrance would we make then?" He huddled under the lintel and wiped a trickle of rain from the end of his nose. "Here's a notion,

Will. You investigate the rear of the house, see if you can find some means of ingress."

"You mean break in?"

"I mean find a way to get us inside before we are washed away in the flood," said Beeston. "You can leave the box with me."

Will set the box of books down at Beeston's feet and looked out at the rain. Bowing his head against the downpour, he stepped out into the storm. As he made his way round the side of the house he saw the blurred outlines of a garden and some straggly trees set out in an orchard pattern.

At the back of the house he discovered a door, but it was firmly bolted. He knocked several times, but – as he expected – there was no answer. Then he looked up and saw above him a small, high window lying ajar.

He tried a standing jump, but his fingers never even touched the sill. Cursing his luck, he cast a look around and spotted a rain barrel, full to the brim and with water spilling down its sides. It was just the thing to give him the boost he needed. With a decisive heave, he toppled it over, sending a tide of water cascading over the sodden ground.

Shaking the rainwater out of his eyes, Will turned the barrel upside down and wrestled it over to the wall under the open window. Mounting the upturned base, he shoved the flapping shutters back and pushed off with a grunt.

His elbows found purchase on the window ledge and with a hefty kick he heaved himself head and shoulders through the gap. Legs dangling, he wriggled forward until suddenly he overbalanced and tumbled headlong into the dark.

Will thudded down on to a hard, earthen floor, jarring every bone in his body. Outside a roll of thunder drowned out his squawk of pain as he tentatively fingered his ribs to check that nothing was broken.

"Not too bad then," he thought. Even bruised and winded, he was still glad to be out of the storm. But what sort of place was this?

He struggled to his feet and gazed around him, straining to penetrate the gloom. He appeared to be in some sort of storeroom, though there was little enough stored here. Lightning flashed again, showing him a table with two broken legs, a small tub of mouldy flour and a pile of moth-eaten blankets.

Not exactly a wyzard's treasure, Will thought.

He put a hand over his nose as the stink of rat droppings pricked his nostrils. With his other hand he felt his way to the door and pushed it open. He stepped out into a cramped, dusty passage and followed a faint, distant gleam to a wider corridor where a few shafts of grey light slipped through the slats of a shuttered window.

Buffeted by the storm, the house was creaking and groaning at every joint. It was easy for Will to imagine the noise as the weeping and moaning of restless ghosts. He wanted to call out for someone to come and lead him through the dark, but he was afraid any voice that answered might not come from a living tongue.

He pressed on, leaving damp footprints and a trail of droplets from his sodden clothes. Passages branched off this way and that, some ending in blank walls, others splitting into more forks or opening on to narrow stairways, some of wood, some of stone. Remembering that a couple of the upstairs windows had been lit, Will worked his way upwards.

As he mounted a final steep stairway, he heard a strange noise coming from above. It was a whirring sound, like the fluttering of a bird's wings but much more rapid. At the top of the stairs he emerged into a branching corridor. To the left the walls disappeared into darkness, but the right-hand passage led to a door with yellow light spilling out from under it. This was the source of the unnerving noise.

Along with the whirring he could now hear a regular metallic grinding, like a pair of knives being scraped together. He swallowed hard and started cautiously down the passage. The wall to his left was covered by faded hangings, to his right the rain rattled on some shuttered windows.

Suddenly he heard a stealthy footfall at his back. A poacher's instincts made Will duck as a heavy iron pan whooshed over his head and smashed a chunk of plaster out of the wall. With a loud clang, the pan clattered to the floor.

Will spun round to confront his attacker. He barely had time to glimpse a pair of malignant black eyes glaring at him out of a round, sallow face when he was seized by the arms and lifted off his feet. Rough, powerful hands slammed him against the wall with a force that made his teeth quiver.

"You're a sneaky thief," rasped the stranger, "but not sneaky enough to outfox Caleb Cook!"

Will tried to protest his innocence, but Caleb Cook slammed him into the wall again and bashed the breath out of him. His heart hammered and a red mist spread over his eyes. If he didn't fight back, this man was going to kill him. He twisted his arms free and locked his fingers around his attacker's neck.

"You don't beat Caleb like that," croaked his sallow-faced opponent, shaking Will's fingers loose with a guttural cry of triumph.

He caught Will under the shoulders and hoisted him off the floor, swinging him about like a doll. Then he gave a mighty heave and flung the boy across the passage. Will hurtled backwards into a window. The shutters banged open and he toppled out into the dark and empty air.

7

The Scarab

When Will dared to open his eyes he was horrified to find himself clinging to a shutter, dangling four floors above the rain-drenched garden. He kicked frantically, trying to swing the shutter towards the window and safety, but the violent wind was against him. His arms stretched like tent ropes and his wet fingers ached from the strain of holding on.

Caleb's face loomed at the window like a baleful yellow moon. "There's the price of burglary," he said. He cast a glance down at the ground below. "I doubt you'll have a bone left unbroken after this fall."

One of Will's hands slipped. Choking back his panic, he

tried to think. "I'm not a burglar," he pleaded. "I'm here with Master Henry Beeston."

"And what's he to me?" Caleb growled.

"He leads Lord Strange's Men," gasped Will. "He's come to see Dr Dee. For the love of God, they know each other!" He kicked at the air again, but that only moved him further away.

Caleb drew back from the window.

"Wait!" shouted Will. His shoulders were burning and his sinews were drawn tight. "We've brought something precious for Dr Dee!" The pain was becoming unbearable and Will braced himself to plunge to his doom. "I-can't-hold-on-much-longer."

A hand reached out and grasped the shutter. With a wordless grunt of disgust Caleb hauled it towards the window. Will threw his legs over the ledge and swung himself inside. He dropped to the floor and slumped there, puffing like a fish out of water. Caleb stared down at him, an angler deciding whether his catch was worth keeping.

"If you've come to bring trouble," he said in his cracked, unpleasant voice, "I'll not be blamed for it."

Wiping the raindrops from his face with a shaky hand, Will looked up at his attacker. Caleb looked to be only a few years older than Will, but he seemed prematurely aged by sheer meanness of spirit. The cast of his features was sour and unwelcoming, and his shoulders were hunched as though he were expecting to be struck from behind.

"No trouble," Will assured him. "Master Beeston has brought Dr Dee some books."

"Books," said Caleb with a sniff. "If less was spent on books, we could buy more oil for the lamps, more fuel for the fire."

He started down the passage, walking in a peculiar stooped gait. "The doctor is this way," he growled over his shoulder, with a curt nod towards the lighted doorway.

Will picked himself up and followed his sullen guide. As he approached the door the whirring noise grew louder and more sinister and he felt the hairs stand up on the back of his neck.

"What's going on in there?" he asked.

Caleb shrugged his twisted shoulders. "It's the doctor," he said flatly, as if that were explanation enough. Stepping aside, he caught Will by the arm and launched him forward as he flung the door open. Will stumbled into the room and almost screamed as a monstrous flying shape swooped down on him from above.

It was a gigantic beetle, as big as a horse. Its pincer-like jaws snapped like a pair of clashing swords and its wings fluttered furiously as it bore down on him. Will jumped back, bumping into Caleb who was blocking the doorway. A rush of air ruffled Will's hair as the monster whirled past, the light of a nearby lantern flashing off the silver-blue sheen of its body.

"Don't just stand there!" boomed a voice. "Lend me a hand!"

Snapped out of his shock, Will saw that there were ropes attached to the huge insect, guiding it in a circular path around the room. He ducked as it swept by again, its jaws chomping, its six legs flailing.

Caleb shoved past and scuttled over to where one of the ropes was attached to a winch. He seized the handle and with a strenuous effort started to crank it.

"You too, boy!" came the commanding voice.

On the far side of the spinning monstrosity, Will could see someone waving him towards another rope that was secured to a hook. As he walked towards it, the voice shouted, "Untie it and pull it taut!"

There was a snap of authority in the words that prompted Will to obey. Loosing the rope, he grasped it tightly in both hands and was almost yanked off his feet as the beetle careered past him.

"Hold firm and *pull*!" came the order.

Will planted his feet firmly and heaved back on the rope.

It fed through an overhead apparatus of cogs, shafts and wheels before attaching itself to the body of gigantic insect. Will's fear lent him strength, for he was sure that if he let go, the beetle would pounce on him and use those awful pincers to rip the flesh from his bones.

He hauled with all his might until the rope was taut, wondering how anyone could have captured this monster. Then the truth dawned on him. As the beetle slowed down he could see it was no living creature, but a clever construct of wood, plaster and paint, as false as the props used by Lord Strange's Men.

He saw Caleb cranking the handle with single-minded determination, reining the huge insect in, while the doctor pulled and pushed at a sequence of coloured levers. As the anchor ropes tightened, the monster stopped dead at a central point above their heads. Its jaws gave a final click, the wings twitched to a standstill and at last it dangled lifelessly in the air.

The master of the house came out from behind his levers and circled the floor under the beetle. He stroked his wavy silver beard as he scrutinised the machinery that held the creature in place. His face was flushed with exhilaration as if the whole exercise had been a huge bit of fun, oblivious to the horrid ordeal Will had experienced.

Steel-grey hair curled up under the brim of his round scholar's cap and a long blue robe hung down to his feet, making him resemble a priest or – Will could not help the thought – a wizard.

"It still needs a few adjustments, Caleb," he said. "I'll give you a list of the parts I'll need."

"Yes, doctor," Caleb answered dully.

Dr John Dee turned to Will as if noticing him for the first time. "And what's this you've dragged in? He looks like he's been mislaid."

"I caught him sneaking round the house," said Caleb. "He says he's here with somebody called Beeston."

"Henry Beeston?"

"The same, sir," said Will. "He's waiting at your front door and I'm sure he'd be obliged if you'd let him in out of the rain."

"No doubt he would," Dr Dee agreed. "Caleb, go and fetch Master Henry Beeston up to the library."

Caleb slouched resentfully out of the room, without a word.

"What are you doing in here?" Will asked.

"Isn't it obvious?" said Dee. "I'm building a giant mechanical beetle. I modelled it on the scarab, the beetle god of the ancient Egyptians."

"I can see that," said Will, "but why?"

"Now you're asking a sensible question," Dee beamed. He headed for the door, leaving Will still gaping up at the huge insect. "I wouldn't hang around here," he advised, plucking a lantern from the wall. "It might fall down at any moment and crush the life out of you."

Will hurriedly followed Dee out the door. As they headed down the passageway, he saw the doctor moving his fingers in intricate patterns, as though he were assembling some device in the air in front of him.

Suddenly he stopped and thrust a decisive finger upward, his face lit up with sudden inspiration. Then he frowned. "No, that won't work," he concluded, brushing the thought away with a sweep of his hand that made his long sleeve flap like a ship's sail.

The doctor threw open a door and stepped into a room filled with jars, bottles and flasks of powder, arranged on a set of shelves that went all the way up to the ceiling. He retreated rapidly, closing the door with a puzzled expression.

"That's not right," he sighed. "I sometimes think I should put up signs."

"I suppose that would help," Will said politely.

Two more doors failed to open on to the correct room, but Dee just laughed. "I know what you're thinking, my young friend. You're thinking that this house surely isn't large enough to contain so many rooms."

"That's not what I was thinking," said Will.

"It isn't?" Dee looked genuinely surprised. "That's odd. I think that all the time."

In fact Will was thinking that Doctor John Dee was the strangest man he had ever met and he wondered what other horrific devices he had constructed. He felt an almost overwhelming impulse to run for his life, but he was afraid he would become hopelessly lost in this unearthly house. Will didn't know about wizards, but he had no doubts that he was trapped here with a pair of dangerous lunatics.

8

Pluto and Proserpina

At last Dee found the correct door. It opened on to a cavernous dark so immense that the lantern seemed to shrink before it in fear. The doctor plucked a taper out of a nearby vase and lit it. As they walked deeper into the library he used it to ignite a series of lamps that were placed strategically throughout the vast room. With each new flare of light more and more bookcases became visible, each ten or twelve feet high. They formed crooked passages that zigzagged this way and that from one end of the room to the other, turning the library into a gigantic maze. Crammed on to each shelf were volumes of every imaginable size, shape and colour.

"There must be thousands of books here," Will gasped.

"I dare say there are," said Dee, "though I've never found time to count them."

The doctor strode on, lighting lamps as he went with scarcely a pause. Will stumbled along after, unable to tear his gaze away from this wondrous array of books. He had not imagined there were this many in the whole world. Running his eyes over the titles on the bindings, he saw that there were volumes on mathematics, astronomy, logic, mythology, saints, falconry and magic. Surely everything that could be known was contained in this library.

"Keep up! Keep up!" Dee's voice prompted him.

Will looked around and realised he had lost sight of the doctor. "I can't see you!" he called back.

"Well, keep looking!" came the response. "I must be around here somewhere!"

Will headed left, then right, straight into a dead end. He resisted the impulse to call out for help. This was only one room after all: he could surely find a way through it.

Then he spotted a ladder set at a steep angle upon a wedge-shaped wooden frame. Obviously it was designed for reaching the upper shelves, but if he climbed to the very top he might be able to spot the doctor over the tops of the bookcases.

Darting over to the ladder, he jumped on to the bottommost rung. To his shock the apparatus shot off sideways on unseen wheels. Rows of books flashed by in a giddy rush and a wall loomed suddenly ahead. Will shut his eyes tight and braced himself.

With a jolt, the framework crashed into the wall, knocking loose two rows of books. Opening his eyes with a sigh of relief, Will carefully dismounted. He began to wonder if this entire house was one huge death-trap.

He knelt to replace the fallen books.

"Ah, there you are!" came a voice from above.

Will looked up and saw Dee's face peering down at him through a gap in one of the upper shelves. "I've warned Caleb not to oil the wheels so freely. One day there might be a serious accident."

The face vanished and a moment later Dee appeared by Will's side. He led the way to the centre of the library, which was lit by three separate lamps. There was a large table here, strewn with books, papers, pieces of crystal and mathematical instruments.

"With all this," said Will, staring about him, "how do you find the books you want?"

"This library is arranged according to a thematic system

of my own devising," Dee explained. "It would take a very long time to explain."

"I'm sure it's very clever," said Will.

He peered at one particular book that lay on top of a sheet of incomprehensible calculations. It's green cover looked new, though the title made it sound very old: *A True Treatise on the Construction of the Labyrinth of King Minos.*

He was about to open it when Dee whipped it out from under his nose and set it to one side. "I can't think what that's doing here," he murmured distractedly.

"Dr Dee?" called a familiar voice from somewhere in the direction of door.

"Beeston, is that you?" Dee responded.

"Right here, doctor. Is my boy Will with you?"

"Yes, I'm here," Will interposed, "wherever here is."

A few moments later Caleb appeared with Henry Beeston at his shoulder.

"No matter how many times I've been here," said Beeston with a shake of his head, "I'm sure I would still get lost in this room without a guide."

"Lost? Not a bit of it!" said Dee. "You simply have to remember to always take the left turn. Or is it the right? Anyway, it's the simplest thing." His eye lighted on the box

Beeston was carrying. "So what's this you've got for me?"

"A few volumes I know will interest you."

"Excellent!" Dee enthused. "Drinks, Caleb!"

"What sort of drinks?" Caleb asked dully.

"Oh, I don't know," replied Dee. "Something hot. Isn't there any of that apple punch left?"

"I'll see if I can find some," said Caleb, shuffling off.

Beeston gazed after him. "I can't think why you keep such a surly servant about the place."

"He's my assistant, actually," said Dee. "There are servants too, but they come and go. None of them stays for long. I can't think why."

Beeston set the box down on the table. As soon as he opened it, Dee reached inside, clearly delighted. He lifted the books out one by one, handling them as carefully as if they were made of eggshells and gossamer.

"Tully's translation of the *Cyropaedia*! Splendid! And what's this? *The Voyage of Prince Madoc*. This is treasure indeed! I'll be sure to pay you double the usual fee, Master Beeston, as soon as I am in funds."

"In funds?" Beeston's smile drooped. "Not now?"

"Sadly my finances are at a low ebb," said Dee absently, leafing through one of the books. "But even now I am taking steps to improve my situation."

"I'm glad to hear that," said Beeston, "but perhaps in the meantime…"

"Where's the rest of your company?" Dee asked. "Not abandoned you, I hope?"

"The wagons were bogged down in the mud," Beeston retorted stiffly. "They'll be here presently."

"In that case, Master Beeston, it's not chance that brought you here but the guiding hand of all-seeing providence." Dee set the book aside and looked up with a broad grin. "I am laying on a very special entertainment in two weeks time and the centrepiece of this revelry requires a troupe of players. I had thought of hiring Worcester's Men, but—"

"Worcester's Men?" Beeston cut in. "You can't be serious! Tunstall can barely speak two lines without spraying the audience in spittle. And as for Dick Andrews, I've seen baboons that could pass for a woman better than he, no matter how much makeup they cake on him."

"Well, there you are then," said Dee cheerfully, as if that settled the matter. "I promise you this will lift Lord Strange's Men to the very pinnacle of fame."

"What's the play?" Beeston inquired keenly. "*Damon and Pythias? Gorboduc* perhaps? My tragic kings are unsurpassed for the extremity of their despair."

Dee beamed. "It's a brand new work of my own."

He beckoned them to the other end of the long table and proudly presented an enormous heap of papers that were straining to burst free of the tenuous cord that bound them together. Beeston leaned over to read the title on the topmost sheet.

"*The Most Delightful Historie of Pluto and Proserpina, the King and Queen of Faeries...*" he paused to take a breath "*...and their Attendance at the Wedding of Theseus, Duke of Athens, with Hippolyta, Queen of the Amazons.*"

"I've adapted it from one of Chaucer's poems," Dee explained, "though, as you can see, I have expanded considerably upon the original. It concerns Pluto and Proserpina, the king and queen of the faerie folk, and how they visit the wedding of Theseus, Duke of Athens, to Hippolyta, Queen of the Amazons."

"I deduced that much from the title," said Beeston dubiously.

"Ah, but there's more," said Dee, his large grey eyes sparkling with excitement. "Pluto looks fair on Hippolyta and Proserpina looks likewise upon Theseus. The discord between them causes an angry storm to rend the heavens with wind and lightning. Theseus and Hippolyta have a falling out over some business or other – I think it concerns a

74

ring – and go their separate ways. Lost in the storm the discordant lovers encounter sundry faeries and other creatures, suffer a variety of transformations, and sing several pastoral songs before finding each other and—"

"It sounds engrossing," Beeston interrupted, "but I suspect it may prove overlong for the stamina of both players and audience alike." He gave the mound of pages a cautious poke.

"Quite possibly," Dee agreed. "I wrote it down as the inspiration came to me and I understand that some degree of editing may be in order. Perhaps you could cast your expert eye over the material and knock it into shape for me."

Henry Beeston took a wary step backwards. Then he turned abruptly to Will. "Young Will here's the man for you. He fancies himself a poet."

"This fine young fellow?" said Dee. "I never did catch his name."

"This is Master William Shake—"Beeston caught himself "...shaft. Yes, William Shakeshaft."

"I never said I was a poet," Will protested.

"No need for such modesty, Master Shakeshaft!" said Dee, clapping an encouraging hand on his shoulder. "It only requires a spot of tidying here and there."

Will stared at the tottering manuscript and swallowed.

Even that might take a lifetime, he thought.

"Let me have a word with the lad," said Beeston, giving Dee a wink. He drew Will behind one of the bookcases as the doctor absorbed himself in his new volumes.

"What's this Shakeshaft business?" Will hissed.

"If word of your illegal activities has by any chance reached as far as London, I don't want it interfering with my plans," Beeston explained. "Therefore it's best if you adopt a 'stage name', so to speak."

"Nobody around here is going to care what happens in Stratford," said Will.

"Nevertheless, from now on you are Shakeshaft," Beeston told him. "The important thing is that we have an opportunity here. I'll wager every important figure in London will be attending these revels of Dee's. It's just what I've been hoping for."

"It's all right for you," said Will. "You're not the one that's going to be humouring this lunatic. Did you see the size of that play of his? I swear it's as long as the Bible!"

Beeston put an arm around Will and drew him close. "Don't think of the work, Will, think of the rewards," he said with an excited sparkle in his eyes. "I tell you, we are standing on the very brink of greatness."

Mortlake, VIIth Daye of August, 1579

Most Worshipfulle and Illustrious Parents,

I greet you from afar by the Golden Light of Phoebus, the Sunne, and by the Silver Glowe of his sister Diana, the Moone. If my language seems strange you can blame it on Dr Dee's playe. All of his Characters speak like this. Whenever one of them opens his mouth I know he will not run out of breath for at least three pages. They are constantly draining cuppes of wine in one draught and setting out for Egypt. I do not know if any of them ever get there for they reappear in the next scene as if they had never left.

At least I have learned the purpose of the Monstrous Scarab that caused me such alarm upon my arrival at Mortlake. Dr Dee intends attaching it to a wire running from the rooftop to the garden below and by this means to create a startling effect at the climax of his playe (I agree that the playe needs all the help it can get!)

Pluto, the Faerie King, will summon the sacred insect to beare himself and his bride away to Egypt. At this point the Scarab will rise out of concealment, to the general wonderment of all, and carry the royal couple by means of the wire up to the highest rooftop of the House.

As Lord Strange's Men rehearse what little of the playe is so far capable of being performed, Kemp continues to try the patience of Master Henry Beeston with his untimely dancing. Tom Craddock has come down with a bad cold and has therefore been judged unfit to portray Proserpina the Faerie Queen. He is sore affronted by this and I can see him biting on his kerchief in frustration as he watches Kit Beeston usurp this important role.

Finding my way around Mortlake House is as difficult as trying to make sense of Pluto and Proserpina. I could swear that the rooms themselves grow discontented with their positions and agree to swap places with one another in the night while we are all asleep. A tapestry that marked the Study door one day hangs outside the Kitchen on the next. The stone Knighte who stood by the second floor staircase now guards the way to the Cellar.

While the rest of the Players have been lodged in the barn and other outbuildings, I have been given a bedchamber in the east wing of Mortlake House. Caleb has a chamber in the west wing, which is otherwise deserted, consisting of derelict storerooms and empty servants' quarters. I encounter him on occasion wandering the corridors on errands known only to himself and have never once known him lose his way. In fact he appears to know the House so well, he can find his waye even in the dark without the aid of a candle.

He tells me that many years ago his family owned this House and the land about it. Unluckily for them they chose the wrong side in too many wars so that those that were not slaine in the fighting lost all they had, the House included. I said they must have been very rich to live in so grand a habitation.

Back then, Caleb tells me, it was much, much smaller. The Doctor has added to it floors, wings, cellars even, so that it's hardly fit to live in any more, he says. Caleb was raised by his Mother in a nearby village and she seems to have made him mindful of his heritage.

I asked Dr Dee about Caleb's mother. "She was an unhappy woman," he tells me, "abandoned by the father of her child and forced to raise him alone. She supported the two of them by mixing medicinal potions out of herbs and selling them. It was on this account she was reckoned a witch and suffered much mockery and ill usage." If such was Caleb's childhood, it is small wonder he is sour and stunted of soul.

Dr Dee explained further that when the mother lay

dying, he himself attended her, supplying what remedy and comfort he could. With her final breath she begged the Doctor to have a care for the boy and see to it that he had some prospects in life. That is why Dr Dee took Caleb into his household.

I related to Dr Dee Caleb's tale of how this House and Land once belonged to his family. Dr Dee says this is just a fable devised by his mother to sustain his spirits through their many hardships. He himself considers it a kindnesse never to reveal the truth to Caleb and he admonished me to keep silence also. I swore I would, but I fear Dr Dee little suspects the poison that is brewing in Caleb's troubled heart as a result of his well intentioned lie.

I must return to my labours now for we have less than two weeks before Dr Dee's mysterious Guests arrive. Master Henry Beeston has impressed upon me the importance of this performance. He says we are playing to no ordinary crowd and hints that the future of England may hang upon what happens here. When I scoff at this notion he becomes more grim than any of his tragic Kings. He warns me that England is riven with deathly conflict and that we Players stand on the edge of a precipice.

I scarcely know if it is true or whether he has become so

accustomed to dramatising even the simplest of things that he imagines dangers where none exist. Nevertheless, according to Master Beeston, some call it treason to travel the country spreading tales of Kings overthrown by their subjects or struck down by the hand of God. "Think on it, Will," says he. "The Churches are now owned by the Queen and her Ministers. There's no place left for dissent but the stage. And if we put a foot wrong, it's the dungeon for us and the headsman's block."

Has England truly become so perilous? If so, perhaps we should take refuge in some peaceful, far-off land. Like Egypt.

May God keepe you all in His care.

Your Most Worshipfulle and Illustrious Sonne,

Will Shaxpear

9

The Goblin Court

"It's murder," said Dee. "Murder pure and simple."

"No," said Will, "all I'm doing is cutting some minor characters out of the play. It's either that or you'll have to hire another twenty players."

"Twenty?" Dee echoed, stroking his beard. "That would prove expensive. These are minor characters you say?"

"They won't even be missed," Will assured him.

Dee made an unhappy noise and turned to adjust a valve on one of his alchemical furnaces.

After days of wrestling with *Pluto and Proserpina* and listening to the complaints of the players, Will had tracked

Dee down to confront him with the problems. He had found him in the spacious, stone-built laboratory at the back of the house. The sturdy construction was intended to withstand any possible explosions from the doctor's experiments.

There were five alchemical kilns in here, each as big as a stove, making the laboratory look like a cross between a furnace room and a brewery. The fires blazed and the tanks bubbled all day long in order to produce a few grains of powder or a dribble of clear liquid.

As Dee continued adjusting his equipment, Will pressed on. "And there's another thing. The songs. They don't make any sense."

Dee looked round and quirked an eyebrow. "They make sense to me."

"But not to me or the players," said Will. "I can't even tell what language they're supposed to be in."

"They are in a special language I devised to communicate with the spirit realm," Dee explained.

"I'm sure that's very exciting, but I was thinking of the audience," said Will. "They won't understand it. They'll grumble."

Dee's voice dropped to a secretive hush. "There's a wider audience than those seated before the stage, Will. There's a world of spirits out there…" he swept his hand through the air in a broad flourish "…and they too can be enticed by the power of words." He leaned close and added with an excited glint in his eye, "If we flatter them perhaps they will reveal themselves to our mortal eyes. Wouldn't that be a wonder to behold?"

"Yes, it would," said Will with a defeated sigh. He realised that the only course open to him was to cut out as many of the nonsensical songs as he could and hope that the doctor wouldn't notice.

There was a sudden bang, and a puff of smoke from one of the alchemical kilns filled the air with a stink of rotten eggs and vinegar. Dee uttered a noise like a startled donkey and flew over to inspect the result of the detonation. Will decided to leave before something worse happened.

That evening he started awake from a dream of fleet-footed beings with wings and horns dancing in a starlit wood. Before him on the table-top lay the heaped up pages of *Pluto and Proserpina*, with a damp smudge where his cheek had pressed.

He stretched his arms with a yawn, letting his eye run down the page before him. Now he knew where his dream had come from. He had dozed off while trying to make sense of one of Dr Dee's 'songs'.

"The only thing this rubbish is going to attract is a shower of rotten vegetables from the audience," he muttered.

Suddenly he was aware of a strange noise, like the buzzing of a bluebottle, but more irregular. Will's first thought was that it was a vestige of his dream, hanging about like a wisp of smoke from a burned out fire. He tried shaking it off with a toss of his head, but it persisted.

Slipping out into the shadowy corridor he could hear it more clearly. It was a weird chant coming from some far off part of the house. The unearthly rhythm sent a chill down Will's spine, but it also pricked his curiosity. In spite of his shivers, he knew he had to investigate.

Step by step he followed the sound, down the passageway and through an arch decorated with the symbols of the zodiac. As the noise grew louder it began to resemble strings of words, but surely no human tongue was meant to utter such barbarous syllables.

Rounding another twist in the passageway, Will found himself standing before a stout door. On the other side the raw, barbaric voice continued its rough chant. Will threw back his shoulders and drew himself up straight. He wouldn't skulk like a thief or a spy. Pushing the door open, he marched boldly inside, braced to confront whatever awaited him.

What he saw took his breath away. There before him sat

a fairy, an ogre and an elf, the candlelight flickering weirdly over their inhuman features. And in their midst sat Dr Dee, looking as comfortable in this extraordinary company as only a wizard could.

"You did it!" Will stammered. "You've conjured fairies into flesh!"

The ogre had broken off his chant the instant Will entered. Now he jumped to his feet and whipped a jagged knife from his belt.

Dee stood up and placed a calming hand on the creature's arm. "Lok, my good fellow, there's no need for that. This is Will Shakeshaft. He's assisting me in one of my endeavours."

The ogre looked from Dee to Will and back again, then sat down with a grunt, thrusting his weapon back in its sheath. The elf prince observed all of this with an air of hearty amusement while the fairy put a dainty hand to her mouth to suppress a titter.

"Come in, Will, and shut the door like a good fellow," said Dee.

Will did as he asked and warily approached the goblin court the doctor had conjured up for himself.

"Will Shakeshaft," said Dee waving him genially forward, "may I introduce you to Madame Thomasina, attendant upon the queen."

The fairy slid down on to her little feet. The crown of her head barely reached Will's belt buckle. She offered a dainty hand. Will took it delicately and bowed low as he had seen characters do in plays when meeting important people.

"He has the manners of a courtly gentleman," said the dwarf-woman, her voice like the tinkling of a bell.

"You're very kind," said Will. He began to suspect that these goblin folk might be human after all – but if so, they were the most extraordinary individuals he had ever met.

As Madame Thomasina climbed back into her chair, Dee presented the ogre. "This is Master Lok, a native of the frozen lands of the far North."

The ogre stood up, his copper coloured face and black bristly hair making him appear even more bestial at close range. His tunic and leggings were sewn together from animal hides and round his neck hung a necklace of bird skulls, claws and teeth. He bowed, touching a clenched fist to his brow as he did so, and bared his teeth in what seemed to be a smile.

Will returned the gesture but kept his distance. "I'm very pleased to meet you, I'm sure."

The elf prince laughed. "No need to be afraid of Lok," he said. "He's only ferocious when there's a need for it, and we're having a jolly little party tonight."

"Lok was singing us a hymn from his native land," said Dee.

"It is how we pray to the sea goddess Sedna," the brutish Lok explained, "when we want her to send us more seals to hunt."

"And this fine fellow," said Dee, indicating the lavishly garbed young man, "is my friend Walter Raleigh." He indicated a handsome young man, his peacock blue doublet laced with silver, a pearl ring dangling from his ear.

Raleigh stood up, towering head and shoulders over Will, and offered a hand. For all his dandified appearance, Walter Raleigh's face had the sun-bronzed look of someone who had seen his share of adventures and there was a sinewy strength in his handshake. As the man released his grip, Will's attention was drawn to an oakwood casket standing open on a small table close by.

Inside was a smooth black stone the size of a bread loaf. The rock was threaded with veins of gold that sparkled in the candlelight. Before he could take a closer look, Walter Raleigh casually flipped the lid shut and pushed the casket to one side.

"And what is it you do around here, Will?" he asked affably.

There was a burr to his speech that told Will he came

from somewhere in the south-west of the country. He had heard travellers from Devon and Cornwall speak with that same accent, but none of them had ever dressed like Walter Raleigh. If fine clothes were anything to go by, he must surely be a very important gentleman.

"I'm helping Dr Dee with his play," Will answered reluctantly, hoping the adventurer wouldn't ask for details.

"Poet, eh?" said Walter. "I've jotted down a few odes myself from time to time. Maybe I'll give you a look at them some time."

Will's heart shrivelled at the thought of more bad verses. "I'm sure that would be interesting," he said flatly.

"I must get back to the palace now," chimed Madame Thomasina, sliding off her chair with a rustle of silk. "Her majesty will be pleased to receive your messages, doctor."

"I also will take my leave," said Lok, bowing.

"Are you sure you can find the way out?" Walter joked. "There are jungles more navigable than this palace of confusions."

"Leave him in my care," said the dwarf lady. "I have it all mapped out in my head."

As the door closed behind the curious pair, Dr Dee directed Will to a chair. Walter fetched a jug of wine and three cups. "Here, take a drink with us, Will," he said, pouring a full cup for each of them, "and tell me about yourself."

"There's not much to tell," said Will, taking a hesitant sip. The wine was so strong it made his tongue burn. "I've been travelling with Master Henry Beeston for... well, quite a long time now."

"Travelling?" said Walter, half-mocking. "Is that what you call it?"

Will shrugged. "It's further than I've ever been before. I'm not sure I want to go any further. Certainly not to that country of Master Lok's."

"He's from the far north of America," said Walter, with a sweep of one long arm to indicate the enormous distance. "His land is a frozen desolation where days and nights stretch on for weeks at a time. His people live in houses made of ice and hunt seals for food."

"I – see," said Will doubtfully. He took another sip, a larger one this time.

"It's all true," Dr Dee assured him. "He was brought to England a couple of years ago by Frobisher's expedition. He was so fascinated by the sailors' shiny coins that they named him after the expedition's treasurer, Michael Lok."

Will noticed that there were various maps and charts spread about the room. "Are you planning an expedition of your own?" he asked Walter Raleigh.

Walter smiled and threw back his cup of wine. "I just got back from one," he said, wiping his lips with the back of his hand. "Storms and pirates drove us back to England, but next time I'll have a better course plotted."

"I was never much good at geography," Will confessed.

"Not good at geography?" said Dr Dee. "But, Will, it's the most important thing in the world. In fact, it *is* the world."

"You look like a sturdy fellow, Will," said Walter, pouring himself a fresh cup of wine. "You might make a brave sailor yourself."

"Not me," said Will decisively. "The stage is a dangerous enough deck."

"When I was your age, lad," Walter said, "I was already fighting as a soldier in the Low Countries, helping the Dutch break free of their Spanish masters."

"When I'm your age," said Will, "I hope I'll have no reason to fight anybody."

"Well answered," Walter conceded. "But don't you ever yearn for a glimpse of what lies over the horizon? I could get you on a ship for the Americas."

Will wrinkled his nose. "Why would anybody want to go there? It's all swamp and savages."

"Is that what you think?" said Walter with an amused

twinkle. "You mark my words, Will, there's good farming land out there, and more riches besides."

"Like what?"

Walter's eyes lit up. "Gold. Mountains of it, so plentiful they use it to make doorstops and buttons. At least that's the tale."

"You don't believe that, do you?"

"I believe I should go look for myself. But I promise you this: one day highways will cut through that wilderness and cities rise from the plains, new Londons, Bristols and Yorks."

The wine was making Will's head swim. Struggling to stifle a yawn, he said, "I think you've a wilder imagination than Dr Dee."

"You're tired, Will," said Dee, getting up to fetch a candle. He handed it to Will. "Take this and get off to your bed. Walter and I have many more things to discuss."

Will said goodnight and left the doctor and his friend to their talk. His legs felt as heavy as his eyelids as he retraced his steps to his bedchamber.

"Master Shakeshaft!"

Will almost dropped the candle at the sight of Caleb's sallow face looming out of the darkness. He had been lurking behind a corner, as if waiting there for Will to pass.

Will recovered himself with an effort. "It's late, Caleb. Why aren't you asleep?"

Caleb glanced shiftily to left and right, as if to assure himself they were alone. "When a man sleeps he misses things. You don't want to miss things here."

I'd be happy to have missed this meeting, Will thought to himself. Aloud he said, "Right now I'm missing my bed". He tried to edge past, but Caleb blocked his way.

"You'll not learn their secret, Master Shakeshaft – not without my help you won't."

Will rubbed his eyes. "I don't know what you're talking about."

Caleb gave him a knowing look. "You are right to have a care in speaking of it. But you know the doctor has powers. Remember the storm that raged when you arrived. It was conjured by the doctor, one of his experiments."

"You can't really think that," said Will.

"*You* must think, Master Shakeshaft," said Caleb rapping himself on the skull. "Why would a man gather so many books if not to gain that which he seeks above all else?"

Will stared at him, bemused. "And what would that be?"

Caleb leaned closer and his voice dropped. "The thing all alchemists seek: the philosopher's stone that turns base matter into gold."

Will had heard of such a thing, but it was just a legend, a fantasy. "I'm sure that's not what Dr Dee is looking for."

"Oh, you know what I speak of, Master Shakeshaft," said Caleb. "It's all in his books, you see. Without them he is no wiser than we are. If you will trust me in this, we can share the riches that are due us."

"I have too much to do already," said Will trying to detach himself. "If you think there's some secret to be found, you'll have to discover it for yourself."

Caleb frowned darkly. "We might have been friends in this, Master Shakeshaft, but if you take his side against me, there's an end to it." He slipped past Will and vanished into the dark.

10

The Mermaid

While Lord Strange's Men carried on with their rehearsals, Will climbed the stairs to Dee's study high in the east wing for what seemed the hundredth time. The script of *Pluto and Proserpina* was stuffed under his arm. Steeling himself for another discussion of the play's "merits", he knocked on the door. At Dee's Latin response of "*Intra!*" he stepped inside.

The doctor was bent over his desk running a finger down what Will could now recognise as an astronomical table. Alongside it were a map of the zodiac and various instruments of calculation.

"What are you doing?" he asked.

"Casting a horoscope," said Dee without his usual enthusiasm. "I'd rather not take the time, but the client is very rich and I'm in no position to say no to a jingling purse. Not with these revels to pay for."

"Yes, the revels," said Will. "Who exactly is this all for?"

Dee gave a guarded shrug and scribbled some figures on the page before him. "Persons of the highest dignity who expect to be royally entertained." He glanced up and scratched his head with his pen. "Have you finished the play yet?"

Will groaned inwardly.

"It's going very well," he forced himself to say, "but I do have one or two questions."

"Only one or two?" said Dee, looking up from his calculations. "You must be dozing, Will. Well, speak on."

Will put down his bundle and teased out the pages he wanted. "This part where Pluto and the others all start falling in love with the wrong people," he said. "Why do they do that?"

"Ah, it's the spirits, you see," said Dee, as though this were a helpful explanation. "A man never knows how they will move him."

Will chewed his lip. "But that doesn't make for a proper story."

"It doesn't?"

Will shook his head firmly. Faced with Dee's expectant stare, he decided to gamble on an idea of his own. "Suppose – just suppose – that some other fairy stirs up the trouble," he suggested.

Dee looked intrigued. "And what sprite would make so bold?" he inquired.

Will took the plunge. "There's a mischievous fellow they tell tales of in the country. His name's Robin Goodfellow."

"And your intent is that he should work some mischief to stir things up?" said Dee, nodding sagely.

"Yes, he flies around casting spells on the king and queen!" Will exclaimed, waving his hands about in the air. "He enchants Theseus and Hippolyta, and all those other people who keep turning up as well!"

Dee smiled at his enthusiasm. "The prospect has some merit," he conceded, "but what's he to say? He has no lines and I've no time to compose any for him."

"I could cobble a few speeches together from the verses I've..." Just in time Will caught himself before revealing that he had cut them. "From the verses I've been saving," he said. "Because of their exceptional quality."

"Excellent!" said Dee approvingly. "You obviously have the matter well in hand."

The doctor turned back to his star charts, while Will glanced around the laboratory. He wandered over to another of Dee's curious devices that stood by the window. It was a curved glass lens the size of a dinner plate set in a wooden casing. This was mounted on a stand so that the glass was on a level with Will's shoulder.

Setting the pages of the play down on a nearby table, he stooped to look through the lens. All he could see was a blurred smear of colour that stretched and shrank as he tilted the lens from side to side. He quickly discovered that it could be adjusted up and down as well as left and right.

"What is this?" he asked.

"It's a perspective glass," Dee replied without looking up from his work. "It makes things far away appear much closer. Well, if you're lucky. Sometimes you can see some of the houses in London from here, but the slightest shift in position and you lose the image entirely."

Will experimented, setting both hands on the frame and adjusting it this way and that.

"If it could be made to work properly," Dee continued thoughtfully, "just think how useful it would prove. Sailors at sea could spot land from afar, generals could spy on the movements of the enemy."

Coming out from behind the lens to peer out the window

Will saw Walter Raleigh in the garden below, conspicuous in his silks and velvet. He was making a showy series of passes with his blade, instructing Henry Beeston and Ralph in the proper art of swordplay. Will returned to the perspective glass and turned it upon the scene below.

First a pattern of mottled greens and browns swam into view, the distorted image of some trees. Next he was presented with a wavering expanse of watery blue. Yes, that would be the Thames, which was rolling past beyond the trees. Will swivelled the frame to the left, then recoiled as a startling image jumped into view.

"By all the saints!" he gasped.

It was a woman, thrust upon his gaze so abruptly it was as if she had leapt out of the glass right into his lap. She was lying prone on the grassy river bank. A white robe sullied with mud clung to her wet body and her damp black hair was plastered over her face. It was impossible to tell whether she was breathing but she obviously needed help.

Will dashed out of the room and bounded down the nearest stairway, three steps at a time. Bursting out the front door he raced across the garden where Walter was beating back a mock attack from Henry Beeston and Ralph.

"Ho, Will! What's the alarm?" called Walter.

"Woman!" Will shouted back without breaking stride. "Lying by the river!"

Beeston and Ralph halted, nonplussed, but Walter's eyes brightened. "Perhaps it's a mermaid," he joked. "That would be quite a catch!"

With two quick strokes of his blade he whipped Ralph and Beeston's weapons out of their hands. The two swords glinted in the sun as they twirled through the air and dropped to the grass.

"And that's how you disarm an opponent," said Walter. Thrusting his sword back in its sheath, he set off in pursuit of Will.

Hurdling clumps of underbrush, Will skidded to a halt at the riverside, his eyes darting this way and that. He could see no trace of the drowned woman. The thought crossed his mind that what he had seen was an illusion, some trick of Dr Dee's device. Then he caught a glimpse of white on the far side of a copse of drooping willows.

In a flash he was on his knees at the woman's side, leaning in close to check if she was alive. Her breasts were rising and falling beneath the flimsy white fabric of her dress and Will could feel her breath soft on his cheek. Her black hair and dark complexion lent her an exotic air, as if she had come from some distant land. Will drew back, his fingers hovering over her face, wondering if it was safe to touch her.

A crash among the bushes heralded Walter's arrival. "Is she drowned, Will?" he asked.

Will pulled back his hand and shook his head. "No, she's alive."

Walter dropped to one knee at Will's side. Stripping a kidskin glove from his hand, he brushed the wet, raven locks from the woman's face. "A *pretty* mermaid indeed," he remarked appreciatively. "One of Neptune's fairest daughters."

The woman stirred at his touch and groaned. Then she rolled towards Walter and spewed up a stream of dirty water. Walter jerked back too late to save his satin hose from a soaking. He shot to his feet. "That's no way to treat your rescuers!" he complained.

The woman's long lashes fluttered, revealing brown eyes so dark they were almost black. Her gaze darted fearfully from one side to the to the other

"Don't worry," Will told her, "you're safe now. What happened to you?"

Her full lips twitched, but no sound came out.

"Perhaps she's running away from an angry husband," said Walter, using the loose glove to wipe off his hose.

The woman rolled on to her back and squinted up at Will. "Husband?" she echoed groggily. "Are you my husband?"

Will's face reddened. She was at least as old as his mother. "No, no, by all the saints I'm not!"

"There's the pity," the woman sighed, "for you're a pretty lad, sure enough."

Walter left off mopping his hose. "Who are you?" he demanded. "Tell us what your name is."

She coughed then furrowed her brow. "I've no name," she murmured, "no name at all. No home, no life."

"You must have fallen in the river," Will persisted helpfully. "Don't you remember anything?"

The woman's eyes flickered and she stared up at the sky. "Only angels," she said sleepily.

"Angels?" Will repeated.

"Angels brought me here," said the woman, her voice fading. "They brought me here to guide Dr Dee."

Her eyes drooped shut and she lapsed back into a deep, exhausted sleep.

II

The Black Stone

Dee's gaze widened. "Angels?" he echoed.

"What the lad says is true," Walter confirmed. "For all the sense it makes."

"She says they brought her here to guide you," said Will.

Walter was carrying a dusty earthenware bottle and two pewter cups from across the room. Uncorking the bottle, he tipped a measure of brandy into each cup. He handed one to Dr Dee, keeping the other for himself.

The woman was laid out on the couch in the front parlour of Mortlake House. Dee scrutinised her face as he gently settled a cushion behind her head.

"Well, I've fished some curious things out of the river in my time," he said, "but none so enchanting as this."

"Somebody else must have fished her out," said Will. "We found her on the bank."

"I'll take the credit for carrying her back here though," said Walter, ruefully contemplating the mud stains on his doublet. He made a disgusted noise and tossed back his brandy in one draught.

Dr Dee pressed his cup to the woman's mouth and coaxed her into taking a sip. She licked her lips and murmured something inaudible.

"Is it true?" Dee asked. "Did angels send you here?"

Instead of answering she opened her mouth for more brandy. Dee obliged and this time she took a full swallow. As her eyelids fluttered halfway open, Walter and Will drew closer.

"I was sunk deep in the cold water, closer to death than life," she murmured. "Then I felt soft hands lifting me up." She spoke in a lilting accent that Will didn't recognise, almost as if she were more used to singing than speaking.

"I was carried through the air like I was resting on a cloud and set down on the grass. Beautiful faces moulded out of light looked down on me. *You're to go to Dr Dee,* they told me. *You're the one that's to show him the way he seeks.*"

Her voice trailed off and she sank back into her slumber.

Beaming with excitement, Dr Dee drew Will and Walter aside. "Did you hear that, Walter?" he exclaimed in delight. "*Show me the way*, she said. This is the sign I've been waiting for."

"She's just a woman," said Walter, helping himself to another brandy, "and one that's been robbed of her wits."

"No, no, I believe she's far more than that," said Dee excitedly.

There was an intensity in Dee's voice that Will had never heard before. Walter, however, remained sceptical. "What? Do you think she materialised out of thin air?" he scoffed.

Dee ignored the question. "Will, how did you come to find her?"

"I was trying out that perspective glass of yours," Will replied, "and it fixed upon her. She just seemed to jump into view."

Dee rubbed his hands together gleefully. "Yes, of course, of course!"

"Why *of course*?" Will asked.

"The lens is designed to capture and expand beams of light," Dr Dee explained, "and in so doing must naturally be influenced by them. The glow of angelic light, while it might be invisible to mortal eyes, would draw the glass to itself as surely as a lodestone is drawn to the magnetic north."

"We can't navigate by angelic light," said Walter dismissively.

"Not yet," said Dee, "but perhaps we are on the threshold of something new and wonderful."

"You don't suppose it could just be luck?" asked Will dubiously.

"There is no place for luck in true philosophy," Dee chided him. "Angels, spirits, celestials powers, whatever you choose to call them, they are all about us, steering a man's fate and tilting the course of nations. And they have chosen to deliver this lost soul to me."

Walter snorted. "I'll wager she's one of those wenches that ply their trade by the docks. She gave ill service and an angry client tossed her in the river."

Dr Dee looked pityingly on the sleeping woman. "If she had a previous life, she's dead to that now, washed clean like the world after Noah's Flood." He thought for a moment then said, "I'll name her Magdalena, after the woman brought out of sin by Our Lord."

"We could call her Maddie for short," Will suggested.

"That suits her better," laughed Walter, "for I'll be damned if she's not mad as a March hare and—"

Abruptly they all fell silent. The woman was speaking again.

"Black stone, black stone, black stone" she crooned over and over again, as if they were the most important words in the world. Dee and Walter stared at each other, and this time Walter appeared just as astonished as the doctor.

"The Black Stone!" he repeated. His fingers clenched the hilt of his sword.

Dr Dee ordered a bedchamber to be prepared for Maddie, then one of the female servants Will had glimpsed flitting about the house changed her out of her wet robe into a night-gown. She was fed hot soup with sops of fresh bread then left to sleep for most of the day.

Will went back to work on the play, inventing ways to weave the country sprite Robin Goodfellow into the action. As he toiled, he found his thoughts drifting back to the rock he had seen in the casket the night before. He had no doubt it was the Black Stone by the way the woman's words had struck Dr Dee and Walter like a thunderbolt. He had not dared question them about it, for their manner had immediately become so secretive he was afraid they would banish him from the house if he appeared too inquisitive.

But his curiosity could not be denied. He took to drifting from room to room on the pretext of hunting for trifles – paper, ink, a fresh quill pen. In this way he was able to track

Walter and the doctor's movements throughout the day. He saw them consulting maps, whispering in corners and disappearing behind closed doors to argue.

Once he even risked standing by the door of Dr Dee's study long enough to overhear a discussion.

"Walter, she mentioned the Black Stone!" said Dee. "What other proof do you need?"

"There's more things learned by simple spying than by talking to angels," Walter retorted.

"Is that really what you think?"

"I don't know what to think," said Walter, exasperated, "but I'm ready to let you steer your course for the sake of what might be gained."

"Riches and fame, eh, Walter?"

"Perhaps a whole world," Walter answered. He did not sound like he was joking.

At this point one of the maids appeared at the other end of the passage and Will slipped behind a hanging tapestry before she spotted him spying. He waited until he was sure she was gone, but before he could emerge from hiding he heard the door open.

Walter and Dr Dee were oddly silent as they came out and when Will risked a peek at their receding backs he saw Walter had a casket under his arm – the very one that contained the Black Stone. Will crept after them, padding silently down the passageways.

The two men made their way to Maddie's chamber and emerged mere minutes later with the woman, a warm cloak wrapped round her shoulders, a dreamy expression on her face. Dr Dee led her gently while Walter followed, clutching the casket so tightly, you would have thought it was stuffed full of diamonds and rubies.

Their destination was the library, which pleased Will. Nowhere in all of Mortlake House were there more places to hide. He slid along the walls of books, keeping several discreet paces behind as Dr Dee led Maddie to a seat in the centre of the room. Will deftly removed a thick volume from a convenient shelf so that he could observe them through the gap.

Opening the casket, Walter lifted out the mysterious Black Stone and placed it on the table directly in front of Maddie.

Will caught his breath. Could this be the magical philosopher's stone Caleb had been telling him about? It was certainly like no rock Will had seen before, but it didn't look like Dee and Walter had come here to conjure up gold.

"Is this what you wanted, Maddie?" Dee asked kindly.

Maddie nodded and reached a tentative finger towards

the stone. As soon as she touched it she stiffened so dramatically it made Dr Dee gasp. There followed a pause so hushed and still, Will almost fancied that time itself had stopped. Then Dee broke the silence.

"What's happening, Maddie? What do you see?"

"Nothing," Maddie answered distantly.

"Nothing?" said Walter. He sounded annoyed.

"Nothing but light," Maddie said. Her voice rose in pitch. "The light – it's filled with wings and eyes, moving and watching, guiding and guarding."

Dee and Walter traded glances. "Ask her for more," Walter said. Will had never heard him speak so softly.

Leaning in over Maddie's shoulder, Dee asked, "Can you see past the light?"

"Yes!" Maddie sounded enraptured. "The angels are carrying me now, away across the sky to some far off place. Far, far away. Oh, I see blue water! It's surely the sea, stretching away and away."

"Can you tell me anything else about it?" asked Dee.

"Yes," Maddie replied with a shiver. "It's cold, it's very cold."

Dee gave Walter a satisfied side-glance and said, "Wait a moment, Maddie. I must record this."

He disappeared briefly into the maze of shelves and

returned with a large green book, locked shut with a brass clasp. He took out a small key that was hanging from a chain about his neck and used it to unlock the book. Then he seated himself next to Maddie with the book open in front of him, a pen and ink ready to hand.

"Let the angels take you further," he said, "and tell me what you see."

Maddie sucked in a deep breath. "White cliffs," she half-chanted, "blocking us in on every side. They're high as castle walls, trying to keep us out."

Walter's eyes were fixed upon her in fascination. His usual air of insolent mirth was quite gone.

Dee scribbled down her words. "And what now?" he prompted her. "Can you see a way through?"

"I see open water ahead," said Maddie. There was a tension in her voice, as if the vision was placing a heavy strain on her. "I see steeples of ice rising out of a misty sea... crystal galleons drifting by on a freezing tide."

"It's Frobisher's Passage, surely," breathed Walter.

"Can you see further?" asked Dee, his pen working swiftly.

"I'm trying," Maddie moaned, "but it's very hard. It's a wilderness of white and the light hurts my eyes. I think I see... I think I see..."

She lay both hands upon the black stone and craned over it, moaning wordlessly to herself. Walter made a move towards her but Dee waved him back.

"Tell me," the doctor urged. "Tell me what you see."

Maddie abruptly shot to her feet, the stone gripped between her hands. Her whole body was quivering now. "It's dangerous to go on!" she gasped.

Dee stood up. "It's all right," he assured her in a calm voice. "You're quite safe here."

"I'm safe nowhere!" Maddie declared shrilly. "The cold is biting into me. It's freezing me to the heart!"

She began to sway unsteadily from side to side.

"This is too much!" said Dee, dropping his pen. He stood up and tried to wrestle the black stone away from Maddie. Her grip tightened convulsively and she bared her teeth like an enraged cat. With a determined heave Dee wrenched it out of her grasp and fell back into his chair.

Maddie uttered a high pitched shriek and swooned. Before Walter could catch her, she collapsed across the table, striking the empty casket with an outstretched arm and sending it clattering to the floor.

My Dear Parents,

This truly is a House of Madnesse and Wonders. I have encountered Monsters, Faeries, Ogres, and now a Mermaid we have named Maddie. I suppose she is not really a Mermaid (that was Walter's joke), but she is the most curious woman I ever met. She has no possessions other than the gown she was wearing and no memory of who she is or where she came from.

I hit upon the notion of clothing her out of the stage garb of Lord Strange's Men and made haste to the barn where the costumes are stored. As I rummaged through the chests, Tom Craddock complained most sorely that these queenly gowns were meant for him and tried to drive me off with a cannonade of sneezes.

After I had given her the robes, she paraded around in them with a playful smile on her lips. "I'm fit to be a Queen, don't you think, Will?" she asks in that curious accent of hers. "Maybe I am a Queen, and if my memory ever comes back I'll return to my homeland to claim my throne."

She is all contradiction, one minute skipping about the garden like a carelesse damsel, the next raging like a half-starved bear over some imagined slight. Just yesterdaye she was passing among the Players as they rehearsed - all smile and lightnesse of step - when Ralph mocked her regal bearing, suggesting that even a boy in woman's garb had more claim to Queenlinesse than she.

She shoots him a look as sharp as an arrow, then seizes him by the hand. With a strength prodigious in a wench, she bends his wrist so painfully he's brought to his knees. She curses him for a milk-livered scut and uses other names you would not wish me to report. Fortunately for the haplesse Ralph, Master Henry Beeston intervened to apologise on his behalf, whereupon Maddie released him and turned all honey-sweet once more.

And so she piles confusion upon confusion, for if she has no recall of her family or her estate, whence comes this hot-tempered pride?

Dr Dee believes Maddie is in communication with Spirits and, as I have witnessed, he has been recording the messages she receives from the Spiritual Realm. His friend Walter Raleigh, for all his worldliness, is also not immune to Maddie's enchantment. However, I suspect it is her physical ornaments that hold him in thrall rather than any communication she might impart from the Realm of Spirits. Young as he is - no more than twenty-four, I reckon - his life is already filled with many Adventures, which he is not slowe to relate, but when Maddie runs a finger down his arm and speakes sweetly in his ear, he appears more confounded than if he were sailing through a tempest into the gaping maw of a sea serpent. Today Dr Dee has dispatched him to London to purchase some charts, but I cannot help suspecting he has sent him away to spare him further discomposure.

Even Caleb, as surly a fellow as ever walked the earth, has fallen victim to her charms. Many times I have spied them huddled together in hushed conversation, and once I saw Caleb's mouth contort into something disturbingly close to a smile. This morning I came upon him slouching down a passageway with a vase under his arm. When I ask where he is taking it, he answers curtly, "I was cleaning it. Now I'm putting it back." He snatches the figurine of a Roman goddess out of a nearby alcove and set the vase in its place. Seeing in this the solution to a mystery that has been puzzling me for days, I asked, "Do you think you should be moving these things from place to place? It might confuse people."

"Where's the harm in it, Master Shakeshaft?" is his reply. "I have my rights in this house after all." He was about to go when I made reference - perhaps unwisely - to his friendship with Maddie. He fixes me with a glowering eye, and accuses me of spying on him. "I gave you the offer of my friendship, Master Shakeshaft," sayes he, "and you spurned it. That lady is quicker of wit than you, maybe wiser even than the Doctor. Oh, yes, I'll have my due," sayes he. And with that he lurches off out of sight.

The brighter side of all this is that Dr Dee is so occupied with Maddie and his researches that he has lost all interest in supervising the preparation of Pluto and Proserpina. Thus I am free to effect the many necessary changes without giving him explanation. When I weary of Dr Dee's verses, I visit the Library and find relief in the tales of Ovid and the comedies of Plautus.

London is only eight miles distant and I fancy there must be many wonderful sights to behold there. Having come so close (it is one hundred miles from Stratford) it would be a shame to see none of them. But my businesse binds me here like a chain and by the time this work is finished, I hope to return to Stratford to see you all again.

So London must await my call.

God guard and bless and keep you all,

Your most poetical Sonne,

Will ~~Shakeshaft~~ Shakspere

12

Curtain Saturday

Will poised his spear and took a deep breath. Keeping his eye fixed on his prey, he struck. The sharp point pierced the surface and glanced off a marbled pebble. The trout flashed by without a scratch and disappeared into the deeper water where he could not follow.

"Clodpole!" Will cursed himself.

For the past half hour he had been stalking barefoot through the shallows of the Thames, home-made spear at the ready. But he'd lost patience and stabbed too soon, forgetting how the water deceived the eye.

A hard morning wrestling with Duke Theseus's epilogue,

which marked the welcome close of Dr Dee's play, had left him exhausted. The speech seemed to drone on forever in language so bloated he could hardly judge what to keep and what to cut out. Finally he decided that if he didn't stop and have some fun he would end up as addled as Maddie.

Fleeing the library for the orchard, he broke a branch from one of the trees and whittled it to a sharp point, as his father had taught him when he was only five. John Shakespeare had trained him to move cautiously so as not to startle the fish, and taught him where on the Avon he would find the most plentiful hunting grounds.

The Thames was another matter. Will wondered if the great river were simply barren by nature or whether some baleful influence emanating from Mortlake House was scaring the fish away.

Disgusted with his failure, he decided to abandon the hunt. Returning to the bank, he was just pulling on his shoes when a splashing from beyond the drooping willow trees alerted his poacher's instincts. He was trespassing on no one's property here, but force of habit made him withdraw into the shelter of the bushes.

Peering from cover, he glimpsed a small rowing boat forging upstream, very close to his side of the river.

The sole oarsman had his back turned, so his face was

hidden from view, but Will noted that he kept casting furtive glances towards land. It looked like he was keeping in the shade of the overhanging foliage so he could not be spotted from the windows of Mortlake House.

From his vantage point in the undergrowth, Will watched as the rower pulled ashore and climbed on to land. The stranger cast a wary look around him. He was a short, wiry man with grizzled hair, dressed in sailor's garb, with baggy breeches tucked into his leather sea boots and a curved sword dangling from a belt that hung crosswise over his shoulder.

Singling out a nearby beech tree, the stranger pulled a knife from his boot and carved a zigzag notch in the bark. Then he took something from his pocket and concealed it among the roots before returning to his boat and taking to the river once more. With the current now behind him, he quickly disappeared around a bend.

Will was intrigued by this elaborate performance. Checking that the rowing boat was well out of sight, he went to the beech tree and raked his fingers through the leaf-mould at its base. The mystery object came readily to hand. It was a small scroll of yellow paper.

Unrolling it, Will saw two words written in a clumsy hand:

CURTAIN SATURDAY

He stared at the writing but could make no sense of it. To the best of his knowledge there was nothing special about the coming Saturday. Certainly he had never heard of a feast day or holiday by that outlandish name.

He decided against taking the scroll to Dr Dee who would most likely attribute the whole incident to angelic spirits communicating information too subtle for human wits to grasp. Walter, on the other hand, would probably just laugh at him. But the message was clearly intended for someone, so wouldn't they be coming to collect it?

Will rolled the paper up again and stashed it back among the tree roots. Then he darted back to his own hiding place to wait and see if anyone else came along.

His initial excitement yielded to boredom as the day dragged on. He risked standing for a few moments to shake the stiffness out of his limbs and it was then he heard the tell-tale crack of a breaking twig. Someone was coming. Will dropped back into cover. A few moments later a familiar figure appeared out of the trees. It was Maddie.

She was strolling downhill toward the waterside. Arms swinging casually at her sides, she made for the shade of the beech tree. Gathering her skirts, she sank to her knees and began running her fingers through the grass. Then she suddenly plunged a hand into the midst of the tree roots and pulled out the scroll.

She unfurled the paper and scanned it intently. A satisfied smile touched her lips and, rocking back on her heels, she rose to her feet and carried the note to the riverside. With nimble fingers she tore the paper to shreds and scattered them over the water. Then without so much as a backward glance she retraced her steps back to the house.

As soon as she was out of sight Will broke cover and raced to the riverbank. The torn fragments had disappeared, leaving no evidence that the message had ever existed.

He wondered if he should report all of this to Dr Dee, but what was there to tell? That he had found a scrap of paper with two ridiculous words on it? That a madwoman was behaving oddly? No, it was best to say nothing. But from now on he would keep a careful watch on Maddie.

He returned to Mortlake House by way of the garden, where the players immediately crowded round him, all of them disputing the latest pages of the script. Tom Craddock's cold was clearing up at last, but Kit Beeston was reluctant to surrender the role of Proserpina, provoking a struggle for possession of the fairy crown. Henry Beeston complained that too many of Duke Theseus's verses had been excised, leaving him insufficient material on which to practice his art. Ralph urged that the play needed more action. "Something to get the audience on their feet," he said.

"I'll deal with all of this as soon as I can," Will promised, backing off.

Then he broke into a run and didn't stop until he had reached the safety of the house. Shoving the desk up against the study door, he slumped into his chair and rubbed his brow.

"Players!" he groaned.

For the rest of the day he did his best to keep track of Maddie's movements. As usual, she wandered randomly about the house and grounds, except when Dr Dee wished to speak with her. Then they would disappear, usually into the library and often with the casket containing the Black Stone.

Will resisted the temptation to observe or listen in on these sessions. The first occasion had been disturbing enough and he felt a pang of guilt at spying on his kindly host. Maddie was another matter, however. He discovered that there was a small turret room she liked to retreat to, and the following evening he worked up the nerve to sneak right up to the door.

It was ajar. Peeking through the crack, he saw Maddie seated on the edge of the open window, staring off toward the west. She was singing softly to herself, and though he strained to hear the words, Will could make no sense of them.

"Se do bheatha, a bhean ba leanmhar.
B'e ar gcreach tu bheith i ngeibhinn.
Oro! Se do bheatha 'bhaile,
Anois ar theacht an tSamhraidh."

The song had a haunting lilt and was in a language he had never heard before. He couldn't shake off the notion that this might be one of the fairy tongues he had heard Dr Dee speak of. Was Dee right after all? Could Maddie really have come here from the world of spirits to reveal some wondrous secret?

Maddie's voice fell silent and she jumped off the ledge with a speed that took Will by surprise. Afraid of being discovered, he darted back down the corridor as the door flew wide behind him. Ducking into a darkened alcove, he pressed his back against the wall and held his breath.

Maddie came traipsing down the passage, humming to herself the same eerie tune. Will made himself still as a statue as she skipped by. Her expression was rapt, as if she were a thousand miles away, drifting through the scented forests of a fairy isle. Then quick as an adder, she seized Will by the arm and yanked him out of his hiding place.

"Ah, Will," she crooned. "You've a fondness for the older woman, I take it. Else why would you be padding along in my footsteps like a jealous lover?"

Will tried to slip away, but Maddie's arm restrained him, shoving him back against the wall He took a ragged breath. "I was trying to find my way to the... the kitchen," he stammered lamely.

Maddie tutted reprovingly. "For a player, you're a damned clumsy liar. You forget, Will, the angels are talking to me all the time and their eyes are everywhere." She wriggled her fingers in the air about his head. "You've been hanging on to my tail for two days now. Should I take it that you're lovesick, or is there something else at the back of all your spying?"

"I wasn't spying, I swear," Will answered weakly. He tried to wriggle loose, but Maddie pressed her body against his, jamming him against the wall. Her breath caressed his face, and he was afraid he might faint. The last time he had felt this hot and weak, he had been laid up in bed with a fever.

Maddie bared her teeth in a smile, a stray lock of her hair tickling Will's cheek. "It would be a shame to rob the world of a bonnie lad like yourself, Will," she whispered, a hard glint in her dark eyes.

A small, sharp kitchen knife flashed in her hand. Will flinched, but Maddie pressed against him even harder to keep him prisoner. With one quick stroke she sliced the top button off his shirt, the blade's edge scraping lightly over the bare flesh beneath. Will swallowed as the point came to rest at his throat.

"You named me well, Will," Maddie crooned in his ear, "for it's mad I am. I'm Mad Maddie and there's no telling what I'll do next."

She stroked his neck with the blade. Will knew if he as much as sneezed she could cut his throat with a flick of her wrist. He couldn't think clearly enough to decide whether to plead for mercy or shut his eyes and surrender himself to whatever she had planned.

Maddie leaned in so close their faces were only a whisker apart. "Aye, Will," she whispered, "you never know what I might do."

Then she pressed her lips hard against his and kissed him. For a few seconds Will's head was as giddy as a ball kicked into the sky. His breath stopped dead, his heart forgot to beat, and his legs turned to water beneath him.

Then Maddie was gone, her mocking laugh echoing behind her as she disappeared down the corridor. Will touched a finger to his throat to assure himself there was no blood dripping from it. His heart resumed its beating and his breath returned in huge gasps.

Pushing himself away from the wall, he made a frantic dash for his room. Throwing himself on to the bed, he buried his face in the crook of his arm with a noise that was half-way between a moan and a sob.

13

The Downfall of Adonis

"Parry left! Now right!"

Will shifted the blunt player's sword from side to side, deflecting the incoming blade. The two swords clashed then separated.

"Now high!" ordered Walter. "Now low!"

Again Will moved to block his blows, each time taking a step back, and another, until he began to stumble over his own feet.

"No, no," chided Walter, putting up his sword. "Space your feet apart for balance and hold your ground. Remember – your defence is only laying the ground for your attack. If all you do is block and retreat, sooner or later you'll be trapped in a corner – and then you're done for."

They were at the back of Mortlake House in a vacant space among the ramshackle outbuildings. That morning Walter had returned from London in good spirits with a packet of papers for Dr Dee. Spotting Will washing the ink of many long hours' writing from his fingers, he insisted on giving him some instruction in swordplay, as he had already done with Henry Beeston and Ralph.

"I doubt I've the talent for war," Will said when they were done.

"Wars come without being wished for," said Walter, making passes in the air with his blade. "You apply yourself to the manly arts, Will, and then you'll write your name among the stars."

"However large his name becomes," called a lilting voice, "it will never be on your lips as often as your own."

Maddie ambled round the corner of one of the outbuildings and stopped there with one hand resting on her hip. Will instinctively edged closer to Walter, as if a wolf had just come padding out of the underbrush.

"Why, my Lady Mad," Walter greeted her, "so the angels have not taken you back to their bosom."

"My Lord Roughly, no," Maddie responded tartly, "they'd

rather keep me here to puncture your pride."

"I would rather trumpet my name abroad," said Walter, pointing at her with his sword, "than have it forgotten, as yours is, even by yourself."

Maddie strolled casually past them. "Your wit is almost as sharp as that oversized needle you carry about with," she remarked.

Walter sheathed his sword and grinned. "I promise I'll take care not to prick you with it."

Maddie disappeared into the house and even when she was out of sight Walter continued to smile after her. Will realised the young adventurer was more taken with the madwoman than he would ever confess to. He needed to warn him just how dangerous Maddie was, even if it meant embarrassing himself by telling how she had caught him last night.

Before he could speak, a window flew open high above their heads and Dr Dee's amiable face popped out. "Walter!" he called. "Those calculations of Ortelius's you brought me are exactly what I needed. Come up and see the results!"

Walter waved to the scholar and the window banged shut again. "That's the end of the lesson then, Will," he said, "but remember what I taught you." He patted the hilt of his sword and went inside.

Will stared at the blunt player's sword in his hand, more toy than weapon. It didn't make him feel much like a man, let alone a hero.

That evening Will sat in the centre of Dr Dee's vast library, reading by candlelight. With all the tales of the world around him, he still went back to his favourite, *The Metamorphoses*. He was re-reading Ovid's account of how Venus, the goddess of love, fell in love with a handsome youth named Adonis. He felt as if for the first time he was really beginning to understand the story. Venus cared so much for Adonis, she lived in fear that some awful thing might happen to him, and so she cautioned him to always be careful.

Wherefore I pray thee, my sweet boy, forebear too bold to be,
For fear thy rashness hurt thyself and work the woe of me.

In spite of Venus's warning Adonis went hunting and was gored to death by a boar. Perhaps, Will thought, he should return to Stratford now – whatever trouble still awaited him there – rather than remain here waiting for something worse to happen.

All at once he realised he was no longer alone. Stealthy footsteps were creeping about the library. Through a gap in a bookshelf Will caught the faintest glimpse of a moving lantern.

Blowing out his candle before it could be spotted, he slid off his chair and under the table. When the light reached the centre of the library he saw a pair of legs in stout breeches and leather boots padding by. They disappeared round a corner then he heard a scuffling noise and a creak.

After a few moments the visitor returned and Will heard the lamp being set down on the table above his head. Those boots certainly didn't belong to Dr Dee or to Walter. Sliding out from under the table, Will stole a glimpse over the edge.

Maddie, dressed in a shirt and breeches, was bent over the green book Dr Dee had used to note down her visions. She was trying to force the brass lock open with her knife, her teeth gritted in frustration.

Will's heart leapt into his throat. He ducked back down, his pulse pounding so hard he was amazed Maddie couldn't hear it. His worst suspicions were confirmed. Mad Maddie was no more than a common thief, tricking her way into Dee's house in order to steal from him. The sailor who'd hidden the message in the tree roots was undoubtedly her accomplice and was probably waiting with a boat to help her escape with her loot.

Will was suddenly furious. She had imposed on the good doctor, and used her charms on Walter and himself. Whatever she had in mind, she had to be stopped. He was bracing himself to challenge her when he heard the creak of the library door opening.

Maddie stiffened and Will seized his chance. Springing from cover, he snatched the book off the table.

Maddie rounded on him like a lioness. Her dark eyes flared and she bore down on him, raising her knife to strike. "Give that up, Will," she warned, "or it's no kiss I'll be giving you this time!"

Will took an unsteady step backwards. "This is none of yours to take," he declared, hoping he sounded bolder than he felt. Clutching the book to his chest, he made a bolt for it. A chair went flying as Maddie chased after him.

"You pestilent cur!" she swore. "I'll fillet your gizzard!"

Will ducked behind one bookcase then round another. He realised too late he had no idea where he was running to. One dead end and Maddie would be on him like a fury. He saw one of the moving ladders and scrambled up, looking for some vantage point from which he could fend her off. Maddie was hot on his heels and caught him by the ankle as he clambered on to the very top of the bookcase.

"Drop that book, you slippery eel!" she warned. She tugged hard, setting the bookshelves swaying like the deck of a ship at sea.

With a desperate kick Will broke free and rolled over the

top of the bookcase. Catching hold of a shelf, he hung off the far side, his legs dangling. With a grunt Maddie launched herself after him and toppled the bookcase over.

Will yelped, lost his grip and dropped to the floor in a shower of books, the pages fluttering about him like birds' wings. Then the bookcase crashed down on top of him, hammering the breath out of him and pinning him to the floor.

Through a dizzy haze he saw Maddie's leather boots step into view, saw her hand reach down and pluck the green book from his nerveless fingers. "You're a good lad, Will," she said, "and the doctor's treated me kindly. For that give him this warning from me: tell him to beware the Devil's Fire."

"It's you the devil will be roasting," interjected another voice.

It was Walter.

Twisting painfully so that he could look up, Will saw a wicked smile on Maddie's lips. "I've no time for a love tryst with you now, Walter. Maybe another time, when I've no other business to occupy me."

"Your business here is done, Lady Mad," said Walter. His sword came rasping from its sheath.

"So you've come to prick me after all," said Maddie playfully. "It's not gentlemanly to bare your weapon in a lady's presence."

"I'll not banter with you today," said Walter. "The book, if you please."

"I suppose I've no choice here," said Maddie, "me being only a woman, and you being so well armed."

She held out the book to him but as he reached to take it, she let it fall. Reflexively Walter's eyes darted to the floor. Seizing on the distraction, Maddie grabbed his sword arm, yanked him in close and rammed her knee into his groin. Walter doubled over with bellow of pain as Maddie ripped the sword from his hand.

"What chance has a poor weak woman against such an accomplished blade?" she crooned. "Why, none at all, surely."

Flipping the rapier over, she caught the blade in both hands, then swung it like a club, cracking Walter over the back of the skull with the hilt. The young adventurer collapsed in a senseless heap. Maddie shook her head pityingly and flung the sword down beside him.

"I'll not unman you by taking your weapon," she said, picking up the green book, "but for the sake of your heart, your liver and the rest of your innards, let's not keep company again."

And then she was gone.

14

The Game is Up

"Damn all wenches to the fires of Hell!" Walter roared, kicking a stool across the room and bouncing it off the wall. He poured the last of Dr Dee's brandy down his throat then smashed the empty bottle in the fireplace.

Will was stretched out on the same couch where they had placed Maddie after first discovering her. Dr Dee had smeared a soothing ointment over his bruises and assured him that in spite of the pain he had no broken bones. Caleb stood in the corner, looking on. Alerted by the crash of the fallen bookcase, he and Dr Dee had come rushing into the library barely a minute after Maddie's departure.

"Intemperate language will gain us nothing," Dee cautioned. He sat down in a large chair and drummed his fingers on the arm.

"You're right," Walter admitted, taking a deep breath to calm himself. "It's just that she made a buffoon of me. I've never known a woman with such fight in her."

"Could her hand have been guided by the spirits?" suggested Dr Dee.

"No," Walter retorted sharply, "not unless the spirits are all Burgundian mercenaries."

"Shouldn't we be chasing her?" asked Will.

"I would if I'd the least inkling of where she's gone," said Walter.

Dr Dee waved his assistant to come closer. "Caleb, I've seen you talking with her," he said. "Do you know what her plans are?"

Caleb shook his head. "We spoke of how to bake biscuits, boil a ham, that's all," he said.

"Go search the grounds then," said Dee. "See if you can find any trace of where she went."

Caleb hesitated a moment, then shuffled out of the room, closing the door silently behind him. Walter checked that he wasn't listening outside before speaking.

"He's a shifty rogue," he said.

"His story was badly begun," said Dee. "I had intended to guide it to a happier ending."

"Still, if he knows something..." said Walter.

Dee shook his head. "I don't believe Maddie would have trusted him with any information that would help us."

"I'd settle for some clue as to who she really is," said Walter.

"So you don't believe she lost her memory?" asked Will.

Walter snorted. "We're the ones who lost our wits, trusting her as we did."

"She was very convincing," said Dee. "Those visions she had when she touched the stone—"

"Told us nothing," Walter cut in.

Will recalled what Caleb had said about the philosopher's stone and wondered if there might be something to his theories after all. Trying to sound casual, he asked. "What stone is this you're talking about?"

"I suppose there's no harm in telling you," said Dee. "It comes from Lok's country. It has unusual properties and it seemed to induce certain spiritual visions in Maddie."

"That was obviously just a trick to get her hands on the book," said Walter.

Dee gave a grudging nod. "You're right, of course."

"She has a colourful imagination," said Walter. "Colourful

enough to spin her yarn out for day after day until she learned where you kept the book hidden."

"Yes, that's so," Dee admitted dolefully. "She must have been fully awake when I thought her entranced and spied on me as I concealed it behind the false panel."

"I still don't know what all the fuss is about," said Will. "What's so valuable about that book?"

"It's better you don't concern yourself with that," Dee cautioned him.

"And this Devil's Fire business," said Walter. "What in blazes is that all about?"

"The Devil's Fire," Dee mused, tapping his lower lip with his forefinger. "Do you suppose there's some allegorical significance to it? A warning against spiritual dangers such as pride and ignorance?"

"No, it's a real danger," said Will. "I'm sure of it."

"It takes great depth of philosophy to be absolutely sure of anything, Will," Dee admonished him.

There came a tap at the door and Henry Beeston entered. "I hear the woman Maddie is gone," he said, removing his cap and toying with it.

"Yes," Dee confirmed, "vanished as mysteriously as she appeared."

"And might I inquire," Beeston continued, "if the

queenly robe she had on loan from my supplies has also vaporised?"

"No, it's in her room," said Walter. "Go take it if you want. I'd give a lot to know where she got those mannish clothes we saw her in."

"Probably from the same man that left her the note," said Will.

Dee and Walter stared at him.

"What man?" asked Walter.

"What note?" asked Dee.

Will told them the whole story of the boat on the river and the message Maddie had retrieved.

"Why didn't you mention any of this before?" asked Dee.

"Because it didn't make any sense," said Will. "It still doesn't. I mean, it's Saturday tomorrow. Is that Curtain Saturday?"

"That was the note?" Henry Beeston interjected. "Curtain Saturday? Just those two words?" Will nodded and Beeston smiled. "I can tell you about the Curtain, Will. It's a place."

"What sort of a place?" asked Will.

Beeston beamed all across his face. "Why, it's the most splendid place in all the world. A playhouse!"

Walter smacked himself on the brow with the flat of his

hand. "Of course, I've heard of it!"

Will stared at him. "A playhouse? What's that?"

"It's a building constructed entirely for the purpose of staging plays," Beeston explained, "with rows of seating for the audience. It's a new idea. Old Burbage built one a couple of years ago and called it the Theatre. If you ask me, giving it a fancy Greek name's only going to put people off."

"But what about the Curtain?" Dee pressed him.

"Ah, now that's Laneman's establishment, built last year. They're both in Shoreditch in London. I don't think there's much love lost between those two fellows, for I doubt London can support two playhouses."

"That's it then!" exclaimed Will, understanding at last. "She's to meet someone at the Curtain on Saturday."

"Meet whom?" asked Dee, his brow creasing in thought.

"That's what we're going to find out," said Walter with a steely gleam in his eye. "Will, would you recognise this sailor if you saw him again?"

"Yes, definitely," Will replied.

"Good. Then you're coming with me to London. The game is up, Will, and you and I are the hunters!"

Mortlake, XVIIth Daye of August, 1579

Dearest Father and Mother,

I have time to write you only the briefest note, but it must be writ, for I think it likely I may soon be dead. I am bound for London with Walter Raleigh and I quake when I think on the perils that lie ahead. Walter has told me many times of his brave exploits, even without being asked, and by his own account, even though he has been fortunate enough to survive those encounters with Storms, Pirates and the Might of Spain, his comrades have fared less happily. He has described in unsqueamish detail how many of them were stabbed, slaughtered and drowned. I cannot help but foresee a similar fate for myself, yet I will not dishonour the name of Shaxpere by giving waye to craven fear.

There is at least this comfort: that I am now relieved of the burden of Pluto and Proserpina. It is almost finished and I have handed it over to Master Henry Beeston to put the final touches. I wish him good luck!

The purpose of our journey is to retrieve property stolen from Dr Dee by Maddie, who has been revealed more Cunning than Mad. Though I cannot tell you the object of our quest, its recovery is a matter of the most vital import. Even now

Walter is pounding on my door, urging me to horse. I call for him to be patient lest he break his fist.

I praye to God to keep me safe, but should I not return, I wish you both to know the depth of my affection for you. Father, you have laid before me a goodly example of industry, invention and courage. Mother, you set me on the road of Godly duty and devotion, and if I have erred from this course, the fault lies in my own nature, not in you.

Say goodbye to my dear friend Hamnet for me and tell him it is well I did not drag him protesting into this particular adventure. But for all that, I do miss his honest company and kindly face.

If Sir Thomas Lucy pursues me still, please see that these verses are set before him:

> Thou might be deemed a lion,
> Except thou art so mousy.
> Thou might be called good Lucy,
> Except that thou art Lousy.

Let these, my last words, be affixed to the gate of his manor that he might ever remember

Your Loving and Affectionate Sonne,
William Shackespere

15

At the Sign of the Angel

On the way into London, Will counted three heads, five arms and something he didn't recognise impaled on spikes at the top of the gate. He wanted to ask who these men were, but his mouth gaped wordlessly.

"Traitors," said Walter, answering his unspoken question. "Hung, drawn and quartered. Their body parts are displayed here as a warning to others of their kind."

"What kind is that?" Will managed to ask.

"Catholics, most likely," Walter replied. "Looking to overthrow the Queen and take the country back into the Roman ways of worship."

Will felt a chill run through him as he thought of the Latin prayers his family chanted behind closed doors and the statue of Our Lady his mother kept hidden under the stairs. Did they risk the same fate by persevering in the old faith?

Passing through the gate, they set out across London Bridge surrounded by travellers making the crossing into the City. Will was seated behind Walter on the back of his chestnut gelding.

"Nobody seems very bothered about those chopped up bodies," Will observed.

"From the looks of them they've been rotting up there for four or five days," said Walter. "People lose interest."

London Bridge was built on arches of square stone, thirty feet wide and twenty feet apart. It opened up before them like a street, with shops and houses rising up to four storeys on either side. Compared to this, Will thought, Clopton Bridge back in Stratford was like a line of stepping stones.

Off to the East he could see the white walls and bastions of the Tower of London. He had heard tales of the awful things that happened there, of a torture chamber in the deepest dungeon filled with unspeakable instruments that could break a man's soul. Will had once heard a Puritan preacher at Stratford market deliver a thundering sermon on the torments of hell, and ever since the thought of torture made him squirm.

Between the Tower and the Bridge nearly a hundred tall-masted ships were crowded into the harbour. Huge mechanical cranes loaded and unloaded their cargo while busy officials scurried about, collecting the custom duties.

On both sides of the Bridge the river was crowded with barges and tiny wherry boats that flitted about like fireflies, delivering passengers to all parts of the city. As they left the bridge and entered the crowded streets, Will saw to the West the colossal bulk of St Paul's Cathedral soaring up 300 feet into the sky.

Walter delivered a commentary on the various sights as they rode northward. All about them wagons rumbled by, peddlers coaxed their donkeys along and street vendors gave out their raucous cries. Eventually they reached the Bishopsgate area where the buildings thinned out and the stink of the refuse that littered the streets began to fade.

"This is the best place in the city for inns and taverns," Walter explained. "There's food, ale and lodging, and no man asks your business. Here's the one for us – the Angel."

He turned the horse into a passage marked with a peeling painting of an angel. This led into a cobbled courtyard where a stable boy immediately ran up to take the reins. Once they had dismounted, Walter dumped his bags into Will's arms and tossed the boy a coin, leaving him to tend to the horse. Grunting under the weight of the luggage, Will followed him into the Angel Inn.

There was a score of large tables set about the taproom, though only a few were occupied. At the far end was a wide counter set out with tankards, jugs and plates. Behind the counter, cutting up a game pie, stood a broad-shouldered, large-chested woman whose ruddy face was topped by a cascade of peppery curls.

"Mistress Swift!" Walter hailed her as they approached.

The woman looked up and beamed, her apple cheeks glowing. "How now, Master Raleigh!" she cried. "I thought you were safely at sea. What brings you back to port?"

"The hope of a good supper served at your fireside," Walter answered with a grin. "That and the sight of your pretty face, Mistress Swift."

The woman rolled her eyes. "Heaven bless you for that verdict if it's an honest one!"

Walter rented them a room and they were soon upstairs where Will was glad to lay down their bags. Walter immediately laid claim to the four poster bed and pointed Will to the sleeping pallet in the corner.

"Shouldn't we be getting on to the Curtain?" Will asked.

"It's only Friday, Will," Walter reminded him. "We'll go there tomorrow for the afternoon performance. In the meantime, freshen yourself up and we'll treat ourselves to a fine supper."

The taproom had filled up by supper time and the food was as delicious as Walter promised. Standing at her counter like a general, Mistress Swift dispatched her servants with jugs of ale and platters of beef, her voice rising above the din like the blare of a trumpet on a battlefield.

Walter and Will were just cutting into a fresh joint of mutton when a nasal voice hailed them:

"Raleigh! I say, Walter Raleigh!"

The cry came from one of a group of men who were seating themselves at the next table. All three of them looked to be of an age with Walter and like him were dressed in the latest fashion.

Walter raised his tankard to salute each of them in turn. "Will, this is Johnny, George and my good friend Edward de Vere, the Earl of Oxford."

"I'm sure I'm very pleased to meet you all," Will said.

The three men ignored him and started questioning Walter about his tailor. Will was aware that something had changed in his companion's manner since these three friends of his had appeared. He was guarded now, his good humour forced rather than genuine.

Studying the faces of the newcomers, Will was sure it wasn't the round-faced George or the nasal voiced-Johnny who had affected Walter, but the third man, Edward de Vere. He was older and more extravagantly attired than his companions, and there was something unpleasant about his dark hooded eyes and the sensuous mouth beneath his black moustache.

As he downed his third glass of wine, the earl's eye lighted upon Will at last. "I see you've got yourself a servant, Walter," he said, "and not before time."

"He's a cabin boy, or I'll be bound," snorted George.

"Will's a friend of mine," said Walter. "I'm planning to get him a place at court."

"Best get one for yourself first, Raleigh," Johnny sneered.

"On the subject of courting," said George, "there's a rumour the French King's brother, the Duke of Anjou, has come to London in disguise to woo the Queen."

"I never listen to rumours," said Walter, "unless they're about me, of course."

"Ah, but he's an ugly little fellow," said Johnny. "Pox-faced and hunch-backed. If he had any decency he'd go disguised all the time."

His friends laughed heartily at the joke.

"Well, knowing how he's hated in England," said Walter, "I doubt Anjou has the courage to come here, disguised or no."

"Didn't you hear what happened to the lawyer Stubbs?" George continued in the same gossipy fashion. "He published a pamphlet saying that the suit is a French plot to ruin England. He was dragged off to gaol and—".

"His right hand was publicly chopped off with a butcher's cleaver," de Vere interjected with relish. He raised his own right hand and made a fist. "Stubbs lifted up the bloody stump so the whole crowd could see and declared he was a loyal Englishman devoted to his Queen."

There was a moment of grim silence.

"I hope we're all that," said George feebly.

Will decided that all three of these friends of Walter were loud, arrogant and stupid. Although they fancied themselves as wits, their jokes were cruel rather than funny. Eventually he was so sick of them he made an excuse about being tired and left the table. It didn't surprise him that none of them paid him any attention.

Collecting a lighted lantern from their hostess, Will marched upstairs and stamped into the bedchamber, still seething with annoyance. Seeing Walter's saddlebag lying on the floor, he vented his rage by giving it a hefty kick. The bag popped open and to Will's surprise a book fell out.

He picked it up and examined it curiously. It was called *The Steele Glasse* by George Gascoigne. Flipping through it, Will was disappointed to find it was merely a collection of satirical verses, but when he turned to the first page he couldn't help but grin. It was headed:

WALTER RALEIGH OF THE MIDDLE TEMPLE IN COMMENDATION OF THE STEELE GLASS

Beneath this was an eighteen line poem written by Walter, recommending the book to the reader. Will shook his head and smiled. Then he noticed that the front cover had an odd bulge to it. Examining it more closely, he found a pocket concealed under the leather with a folded sheet of paper fitted inside.

Will slipped it out, supposing it was another of Walter's poems, or perhaps a letter of thanks from George Gascoigne, the author of *The Steele Glasse*. When he unfolded it he was surprised to find a map. It was not a sea chart but the layout of Mortlake House and its grounds. Most particularly marked were the spots picked out for the performance of the forthcoming play and the area where Dr Dee intended to seat his guests.

It was puzzling enough that Walter should want to make a plan of all this, but more worrying was the fact that he had labelled certain locations as being "of goodlie concealement". Not only had he pinpointed these hiding places, he had sketched a broken line showing a route from the river to the house that was shaded from view by trees and bushes, so that a party of men could approach without being seen.

Worst of all, the area where the guests would be seated was marked with a crown. That could mean only one thing: Queen Elizabeth herself would be attending the performance! Much as Will hated to believe it, he could draw only one conclusion.

Walter Raleigh was a traitor.

16

Meta Incognita

Will replaced the map and the book and paced the floor anxiously. What was he to do? He thought long and hard about running back to Mortlake and telling all to John Dee, but for all he knew the doctor himself was in on the plot.

At the sound of footsteps on the stairway he threw himself down on his pallet and pretended to be asleep. He opened his eyes the merest crack as the door opened and saw Walter enter with Edward de Vere close behind.

"Stay out there, Edward," said Walter in a hushed voice. "I don't want to risk waking the boy."

"Be quick then," said de Vere. "I'm not used to being kept waiting in doorways."

Will kept up his pretence of sleep as Walter crossed the room and took the map from its hiding place. Returning to the door, he handed it over to de Vere.

"This is a fine service you're doing," said the earl in an oily drawl. "My friends will be very appreciative."

"Just make sure my name isn't mentioned," Walter cautioned him.

"Oh, I'll keep you out of trouble as surely as I will myself," said de Vere. "Let somebody else take the chances. Still, what a jape it's going to be, eh?"

"You should go now before somebody spots you," said Walter, closing the door.

"You worry like an old woman," de Vere chuckled from the other side before heading back downstairs.

Tossing his sword belt on to the bed, Walter leaned over a porcelain basin and splashed his face with water. Will was so filled with disgust that he could hardly keep still. Was there no end to the deceit going on around him? Right then he made his decision. He would confront Walter, however dangerous that might prove.

Rising silently, he edged towards the bed until his hand was in reach of the sword. Goaded by the certainty that this was his only chance of forcing an answer, he slid the blade from its scabbard and pointed it at Walter.

Alerted by the rasp of steel, Walter turned. He stared at Will for a long, hard moment, then he carefully folded the towel and set it down on the table.

"I've had my fill of being threatened with my own sword," he said with cold anger. "But I suppose it's my own fault for teaching you to fence."

Keeping Walter at bay with the rapier, Will pulled the book out of the saddlebag and waved it in front of him. "I found the map you hid here," he said, his voice shaking. "The one you gave to de Vere."

Raleigh's eyes narrowed dangerously and he took a step closer.

Will swallowed. "Stay back," he warned. "I'm not play-acting, Walter."

"I hadn't reckoned you for a spy, Will," Walter said.

"I found it by accident," said Will, "and I can't unsee it now." He tossed the book down at Walter's feet. "Are you planning an attack against the Queen? Tell me the truth"

Walter bent down slowly and picked up the book. He tapped it impatiently against the palm of his hand. "I'm telling you to put down that sword and let this alone," he said. "It's not what it looks like."

"It looks like treason," said Will. The word seemed to burn his tongue as he spoke it.

Walter fixed him with a steely stare and gestured at him with the book. "I am a loyal servant of the Queen, Will. You should look to yourself before you go accusing your friends."

There was a threatening edge to his voice that struck Will like a glove across the cheek. "What are you talking about?"

"You answer tardily to the name Shakeshaft," said Walter, moving closer, "from which I guess you've only recently assumed it. You cross yourself and call upon the saints for help, sure signs that you've been raised in the Roman religion. Take my word – of the two of us, it's you that's most likely to be taken for a traitor."

"That's mad!" Will declared indignantly. "I'm no traitor!"

"Oh no?"

In a lightning move Walter lunged at him. Beating the blade aside with the leather bound book, he punched Will hard in the jaw, knocking him straight back into the wall. Stunned, Will slumped to the floor and dropped the sword.

"I think you're right, Will." Walter's voice sounded like it was coming from the far end of a long tunnel. "I think it's time we know where we stand."

Will rubbed his jaw and fought through the haze. As his

mind cleared he saw that Walter had picked up the sword and set the point only inches from his heart. Slowly he pushed himself up on to his feet, his back pressed against the wall for support.

"I suppose you're going to kill me to protect your secret," he said, struggling to keep his voice steady, "but you'll have to live with the shame of it."

Walter tapped the sword point lightly against Will's breast, then he sighed and lowered the blade. "I'm not going to kill you, Will. Your intent was honourable and you had the courage to square up to me like a man. So talking as one man to another, I'm warning you to forget all this."

He walked back to the basin, dipped the towel in the water and tossed it to Will. "Press that to your jaw to help the swelling."

Will dabbed his face with the towel, the cool wetness helping him shake of his dizziness. "Are you telling me I have no reason to be suspicious?" he asked.

"No," Walter replied, "I'm saying there are plots within plots and you have no idea what a badger's den you're poking your nose into."

"All I know is that you've been playing a part," said Will, "just like Maddie."

"Everyone plays a part of some sort," said Walter, "just as

you've been doing. All I ask of you is that you trust the honesty of my intent."

In his heart Will knew he wanted to believe Walter was innocent. "I might do that," he said, "if you would trust me in return. Tell me why we came to London. What's so important about that book Maddie stole?"

Raleigh searched Will's face for almost a full minute, then walked right up to him. He upended his sword, holding the hilt between them like a cross. "Swear," he said. "Swear that you won't repeat any of this and I will tell you."

Will touched the fingers of his right hand to the sword. "I swear by God, by our Saviour, Jesus Christ, and anything else you like," he said.

Walter nodded. He picked up the scabbard, sheathed the sword and laid it back on the bed. Will waited in silence while his companion paced the floor, collecting his thoughts.

"The title of the book is the *Meta Incognita*," Walter said at last. "Have you enough Latin to translate that?"

"It means The Unknown Boundary," said Will after a moment's thought.

"That's right. The name refers to what some would call the very end of the world – the frozen sea that lies beyond the northernmost shore of America."

"Is that where you plan to look for the Philosopher's Stone?" Will asked.

"Good God, no!" said Walter. "Where on earth did you get that idea from?"

Will swallowed his embarrassment. "Never mind. Just tell me about the *Meta Incognita*."

Walter picked up his book and turned it over in his hands as he spoke. "For years Dr Dee has gathered charts, journals, legends, everything that will help him map the northern coast of America. Piece by piece he has put together all the clues that lead to the North West Passage. That's what's recorded in the book."

Will concentrated, remembering the maps he had seen in Dr Dee's library and how they faded into blank nothingness to the north of the New World. "There's just a big empty space up there," he said.

"Only on the maps we have now," said Walter. "In reality it's a twisting maze of islands and floating ice. The Northwest Passage is a route through that maze to the Pacific Ocean and the riches of China and India."

"So it's about money," said Will.

"No, not money," said Walter vehemently. "Empire! Both Spain and France would pay any price to possess the New World, but if we have control of the Passage and enough ships to dominate the sea, it will belong to England. America will be our empire."

Will sat down on the bed, trying to contain the whole picture in his aching head. "If all this is so secret, how did Maddie know about the *Meta Incognita*?"

"Dee receives visitors from all over Europe," said Walter. "One of them must have got wind of what he was up to and passed that information on to our enemies."

"And you think they've paid Maddie to steal the book for them."

"They'll do a lot more than steal to possess the secret of the Passage," said Walter. "They'll kill for it!"

"And if we find Maddie at the Curtain tomorrow?"

"Steel yourself, Will," Walter told him. "If it comes to it, we must be ready to kill too."

17

Fallen on Hard Times

"Come see Warwick's Men perform the appalling tragedy of *Murderous Michael* at Mr Burbage's Theatre today! If you have tears, prepare to shed them! If you have blood, it will curdle at the monstrous misdeeds of *Murderous Michael*! Lust, Slaughter and Revenge – all new today at Mr Burbage's Theatre!"

The crier was also waving a bill in his hand proclaiming the play's gory magnificence and he was drawing a lively mob into the playhouse. The Theatre was a giant drum of a building, three storeys high, set in the grounds of a demolished priory. A gaudy flag fluttered above its roof, but Will could see nothing of the interior.

Further off, a sombrely clad Puritan preacher was denouncing the show. "Do not soil your souls with these lewd entertainments!" he admonished the passers-by. "It's naught but painted wantons, godless obscenities and vices exceeding the depravity of pagan Rome!"

"I wish we could go and see that," said Will.

Walter finished tethering his horse to a post and tossed a penny to a ragged boy who had promised to guard the animal "with my very life, sir". He glanced over at the people filing into the Theatre and shook his head. "You'd think they see enough executions not to be impressed by fake bloodshed."

"It sounds a lot better than *Pluto and Proserpina*," Will muttered.

Three short trumpet blasts from the Theatre pierced the afternoon sky and gave an extra spur to the crowd pressing into the playhouse.

"What was that?" Will exclaimed. "An alarm?"

"It means the play's about to start," said Walter. He hooked a hand round Will's arm and tugged him away. "Come on, we're going this way."

They struck out for the Curtain which stood a few hundred yards south of the rival playhouse. It was similar in construction, but not so large, Will judged, nor so extravagantly painted.

"It's an awful long way to come for a play," said Will. "We must be at least a mile outside the city."

"That's the point," said Walter. "The Lord Mayor's a bit of a Puritan, and if he had his way, he'd see both these places shut down. Burned down even. But his authority doesn't extend beyond the city walls."

"Do you know what's playing at the Curtain?" Will asked.

"No play, I'm afraid, Will. The Curtain's fallen on hard times. Now stick close to me and watch out for pickpockets."

They joined a smaller but equally lively crowd that was filing into the Curtain. Walter paid two pennies to a pair of thickset ex-soldiers who admitted them to the entrance passage. From brief shadow they emerged into bright sunlight and a jostling, roaring crowd.

All about them were working folk in stained aprons, countrymen in their coarse, homespun smocks, pimple-faced boys and toothless old men. Wending their way through this boisterous assembly were hawkers peddling baked apples, nuts and beer. The sandy ground at their feet was already littered with fruit peel and nutshells.

Directly ahead was a raised stage projecting out of what looked like a tall, wooden house. Henry Beeston had explained to Will that this was called the 'tiring house', and it was where the actors stored their props and changed costumes. Ringing the stage and the open forecourt was an encircling array of viewing galleries.

"A third hit!" exclaimed a voice from the stage. "A third hit and victory to Master Benjamin Wright!"

There was a thunder of applause and all through the teeming crowd money changed hands as bets were paid off, a few coppers here, elsewhere whole purses of cash. Up on the stage two fencers bowed and waved. A third man standing between them encouraged more applause as the swordsmen retired through a pair of doors to their rear. As they disappeared into the tiring house, Will noticed that one of them was clutching a wound in his side.

"What sort of a show is this?" he asked.

"When money's tight it's a lot cheaper to put on fencing bouts than plays," replied Walter. "No actors, costumes or props, and no writers to pay either – just men with swords showing off their skill to win a small purse and a few cheers."

"One of them was bleeding," said Will. "Are they trying to kill each other?"

Walter shrugged. "They're supposed to fight with blunted swords, but who'd pay good money to see that? The president up there sees to it that nobody comes to serious harm. Well, most of the time."

Will lifted his gaze to the three tiers of galleries where seats were provided for those willing to pay more than a single penny. Here fat merchants rubbed shoulders with foppish young men, and painted women in low cut gowns preened themselves as if they were part of the show. Some even occupied private boxes that were separated off from the rest of the spectators.

"Couldn't we afford a couple of those seats?" Will asked. "We'd have a better view from up there."

"We'd be more conspicuous too," said Walter, "and we don't want to be spotted. You keep an eye peeled for your sailor friend – and for that woman."

The president waved the crowd to silence and announced, "Our next bout is a ferocious contest between two champions of those most warlike nations, Wales and Italy!"

This brought cheers and laughter which redoubled when the two fencers appeared, each through his own door.

"A word, please, a word!" cried the president, quelling the noise. He pointed at a big, barrel-chested man in military boots. "Here on my left stands that indomitable warrior, that Alexander of the valleys, Sergeant Owen Fluellen!"

This brought a roar and shouts of, "Go to it, Welshman!"

"And on my right," the president continued, "the mystery man from Mantua, that belligerent bravo, Graziano!"

The applause for the Italian was less enthusiastic. Somebody yelled, "Send him back home to fence with the Pope!"

The slightly-built Italian bowed graciously. He wore a jerkin of black leather over a green shirt and beneath his wide, floppy hat his face was hidden behind a red mask. Walter explained that many of the fencers chose to keep their true identities a secret.

"Gentlemen, take up your places, please!" the president instructed.

The fencers drew their swords and fell back to opposite ends of the stage to await the president's signal. On all sides Will could hear bets being traded, mostly favouring Fluellen.

A lumpish fellow standing directly behind Will took a swig of beer and burped noisily in his ear. "I've seen Fluellen fight before," he chortled. "He'd be a fool that wagers against him."

"Thanks for the advice," said Will, stepping away.

The president raised a red kerchief in the air, held it aloft for a count of ten, then whipped it down dramatically. The crowd bellowed encouragement as the fighters closed with each other and the president retreated to a safe distance.

Each fencer made a series of feints, trying to draw out his opponent, then Graziano bounded nimbly forward, extending his sword arm in an athletic lunge. Fluellen beat the Italian's blade aside, but did not move quickly enough to avoid a lightning riposte from his opponent.

"Halt!" called the president. "I perceive a hit in favour of Signor Graziano!"

"Curse your eyes!" spat Fluellen. "He struck the empty air and naught else!"

The president took the Welshman by the arm and poked a finger through a rent in his sleeve. "A hit, as I say!"

Fluellen conceded with a disgruntled growl and the fencers returned to their starting places.

Walter nudged Will in the ribs. "Observe the crowd," he said. "We're not here for the show."

As the spectators cheered the swordsmen on, Will swept his gaze around the galleries, hoping to spy Maddie's sailor accomplice. He could scarcely believe it when his eye hit upon the very man he was searching for. The same wiry frame and grizzled hair, the same clothes even.

He was standing in one of the private boxes beside another man, who lounged at his ease in a cushioned chair. The seated man was richly dressed in a black velvet doublet laced with silver thread and a scarlet cloak that hung from his left shoulder. An emerald earring flashed from under his curling black locks as he followed the contest with an expert eye.

Will gave Walter a poke. "There!" he said, pointing up at the gallery. "That's him with the belt across his shoulder."

Walter caught at Will's arm. "Careful!" he muttered. "We don't want to be spotted."

"I don't know who the other man is."

"I do," said Walter. "I met him once at a banquet. He's Don Bernardino de Mendoza, the Spanish ambassador."

"You were right then. He must be here for the *Meta Incognita*."

At that moment the president declared victory for the Italian, Graziano, and the crowd yelled their congratulations. As the cheers echoed around the playhouse, the ambassador stood up and followed the sailor out of the box towards the end of the gallery.

"Now what's this?" Walter exclaimed. "Where are they off to?"

"It looks like they're headed into the tiring house," said Will.

"Then we'll after them," said Walter, clapping a hand to his sword, "even if we must go against the might of Spain."

18

Crossed Swords

To the left of the stage a small staircase led to the tiring house. Walter elbowed his way through the crowd towards it like a galleon ploughing through a sea of flotsam with Will pressing along in his wake.

The adventurer took the three steps in one bound. At the top he pulled his sword half out of its sheath and thrust open the door. Will followed him into the tiring house where the narrow windows admitted a few thin shafts of sunlight.

Off to his right Will could see the two doors leading out on to the stage. From beyond them he could hear the excited hubbub continuing after the last fencing match. A passage leading to the back door divided the house into two curtained areas. The curtain had been pulled back from the closer half, which served both as a dressing room for the fencers and as a surgery. No one paid any attention as the two newcomers made their way along the edge of the gathering.

A physician was busy bandaging up the man Will had seen wounded in the earlier match. Fluellen was also there, thirstily gulping down a jug of wine as he watched a fresh pair of fencers limbering up.

"Show some spirit, by God!" he urged them contemptuously. "You'll be taken for a pair of milkmaids."

There was no sign of Graziano and Will assumed the Italian must have made off with his winnings. In vain he looked around for some trace of the Spanish ambassador and the sailor.

"Where could they have gone?" growled Walter.

"Maybe behind that other curtain there," Will suggested.

Walter put out a stealthy hand and plucked the curtain back a few inches. From inside came a subdued murmur of voices too indistinct to make out. Squinting into the shadows, Will saw that this was where the playhouse's props were stored.

There were pillars made of hollow plaster, small trees

fixed to bases, and a horse made of patchwork and wood. Bushes, thrones, banners and folded tents were piled on top of each other in great mounds. There were even fragments of a ship heaped together like the debris of a wreck.

Crouching down, Walter motioned Will to stay close. Bent double, they crept through the mounds of stage equipment, following the sound of voices. Taking cover behind a wooden dragon with painted fire coming from its mouth, they peered out at the speakers.

Ten paces away stood a table laid out for a stage banquet with platters of fish and fruit moulded out of plaster. Gathered round the table were the sailor, the ambassador and Graziano. Hanging on the wall behind them was a painted cloth showing the city of Rome, lending a grandiose backdrop to their furtive meeting.

Will blinked, wondering what role the Italian swordsman could possibly be playing in this venture. He craned forward to hear what they were saying.

"I would not be so foolish as to carry such a large sum of gold on me when meeting with a notorious pirate, Signora O'Malley," Mendoza stated bluntly in barely accented English. "Show me the book first and I will send for your money."

The sailor spat on the floor in disgust. "I warned you not

to trust him, Grace!" He pulled out a dagger. "Should I carve my name on him for a keepsake?"

"I came here to do important business," Mendoza sneered at him, "not to listen to your cut-throat bravado."

"Quiet, Donal!" Graziano told the sailor. "We're all friends here."

He swept off his hat, sending a cascade of long back hair tumbling down over his shoulders. Then he plucked off his mask and flashed a wickedly familiar smile.

Will stifled a gasp of amazement. Graziano was Maddie! And there was a bigger surprise to come.

"I'm a blockhead for not seeing it, Will!" Walter hissed through his teeth. "Our mad Maddie is Grace O'Malley, the Irish pirate queen."

"Pirate queen? Are you serious?"

Walter nodded grimly. "She and her cut-throats are the devil's own crew. She's buried more men than the plague, her husbands included."

Will fingered to his throat, remembering how close he had come to joining Maddie's other victims.

"Come, cease this womanish coyness," said Mendoza. "Produce the book and let us settle our business."

"Woman or no, I'd be as brainless as a barnacle to have it on me, would I not?" Grace O'Malley retorted.

"Is this just caution or something else?" asked the Spaniard.

"I was thinking," said Grace, "now I have my hands on it, that the price you offered hardly matches so precious a treasure."

Mendoza bristled. "The price was agreed."

"That's surely true," said Grace, "but as you pointed out yourself, I'm a pirate, and I've a reputation to think of."

Donal chuckled, drawing an icy glare from the Spaniard.

Walter tensed, one hand gripping his sword hilt. Before Will could ask what he intended to do, a loud Welsh voice boomed out from behind them.

"Ho there! What are you knaves up to, skulking there in the shadows?"

It was Fluellen, his face flushed with wine, waving the jug as if it were a weapon. Grace's sword leapt into her hand. "Who's there?" she challenged, striding towards the wooden dragon.

Walter jumped up and pushed the Welshman aside. "Damn you, you loggerheaded lump!" he cursed, sweeping his sword from its sheath.

"Walter Raleigh!" Grace exclaimed. She clucked her tongue like a scolding mother. "Did I not already teach you the folly of drawing on me?"

"It's my turn to give you a lesson today," said Walter, "unless you've the sense to surrender."

Grace laughed and cast a sidelong glance at the ambassador. "You'd best withdraw, Signor, while I clout this overdressed blusterer."

With a sweep of his crimson cape, the Spaniard disappeared among the mountains of props. Sidestepping the banqueting table, Donal drew his curved sword.

Fluellen gaped at Grace in disbelief. "A wench?" he moaned. "Oh no, let no man say Fluellen was bested by a wench!"

"Draw, man!" Walter urged him. "These are the enemies of your country!"

"I've already trounced that brabbler, Walter," Grace taunted. "Let's see if you've more fight in you."

She lunged at Walter, her sword point flickering like quicksilver. Walter whirled his blade round in a flashing arc to meet her attack and the two swords collided with a resounding clang.

"Very deft," said Grace. "But how long can you keep it up, I wonder?"

She lunged again and Will winced at the harsh clatter of steel on steel.

Fluellen drew his sword and shook it at Donal. "I'll thank

173

you to keep clear and let them fight fair!"

"Away with you, you sot," Donal barked, "before I stick you like a hog!"

Fluellen tossed away his jug and struck a heroic pose. "Villain!" he declared. "Now you'll know what it is to stir the temper of a Welshman!"

He marched straight at Donal and the two men squared off, their blades dipping and darting.

Still concealed behind the dragon, Will looked around for something he could use as a weapon. There came a steely chime as Walter and Grace matched blows again. The pair of them stepped back to catch their breath.

"You've more fire in your blade than I would have credited after our last encounter," Grace complimented her opponent.

"And you wield a sword like I never thought a woman could," Walter returned. "If you'll give up the book to me, then, as a mark of respect, I'll let you flee."

"Flee?" Grace exclaimed. "You arrogant lout! I'd as soon run from a gnat!" She snatched a plasterwork trout from the banqueting table and flung it at Walter's head. As he ducked the missile, she renewed her attack with redoubled fury.

Meanwhile Fluellen was being forced back by Donal's assault. Step by step he retreated until he collided with a towering heap of wooden planks and gaudy tents. Before he could make a move to escape, the whole mass of it came crashing down, burying him under a mountain of theatrical rubble.

Leaving the Welshman groaning, Donal whirled about to strike at Walter's back.

19

Fair Foes

Seeing Fluellen's sword arm sticking out of the debris, Will leapt out of hiding. Making a dive for the weapon, he yanked it from the Welshman's limp fingers. Donal was weaving this way and that, poised to strike at Walter's unguarded back, when Will took him by surprise. Lashing out with Fluellen's sword, he dashed the pirate's blade from his grasp. It flew end over end through the air and clattered out of sight under the table.

Donal rounded on Will and whipped a dagger from his belt. "Are there a score of you whoreson rats lurking about here?" he snarled.

He made a vicious sidearm slash. Will stumbled backwards and only just managed to deflect the blow. Donal closed swiftly, his dagger flicking out like an adder's tongue. Will parried clumsily – left, right, left – then recoiled as the pirate's blade slashed the front of his jerkin.

"Will, remember what I taught you!" Walter called.

"Look to you own guard, Walter!" Grace advised, aiming a thrust at his belly. Walter jerked away just in time and beat her blade back.

If all you do is defend, Will remembered, *you'll be forced into a corner*. This was no time to be a frightened boy, he realised. He must play the part of Robin Hood when he challenged the evil sheriff as he had seen Ralph perform it. He would make Robin's courage his own.

With a wordless cry of defiance he planted his feet. Gripping the sword in both hands he rammed the blade forward into the dagger's path. The meeting of blades jarred him to the elbow, but it was Donal who fell back.

That tiny victory lit a fire in Will's heart. "Have at you then," he yelled, repeating Robin's own battle cry, "and God's curse on him that flees!"

He charged forward, wielding the sword like a flail. Caught off balance, Donal reeled back and stumbled into the wooden dragon.

"Now, Will! Strike!" Walter yelled as he beat at Grace's blade.

Acting on pure reflex, Will drove his sword point straight at the pirate. Donal flinched aside, escaping by an inch as Will's blade buried itself up to the hilt in the soft wood. He tied to pry it loose, but it was stuck fast.

Seeing his enemy disarmed, Donal renewed his attack. Will dodged and scrambled away, cursing his bad luck.

"Run, Will! Raise the alarm!" Walter cried.

Will needed no further urging. He took to his heels crying, "Spies! Pirates!"

"After him, Donal!" Grace ordered her man.

Will wove a nimble path among the towers of props. Behind him he heard Donal's blundering pursuit. Seeing the curtain ahead, he charged blindly through, bowling over the physician who had come to investigate the commotion. Next instant Donal flung himself into the curtain and was caught up like a fish in a net.

Will scrambled clear as the pirate's dagger ripped through the thin cloth and his crimson face poked through the rent.

"I'll have you now!" Donal threatened.

Will made a dash for the nearest door and crashed right through. To his amazement he found himself stumbling across the stage with a multitude of flabbergasted faces staring up at him.

"Away with you, boy!" said the president, shooing him off. "We've a match about to start."

Before Will could even turn round, Donal burst through the door and bashed into him. They hit the stage in a rolling tangle of limbs to the delighted hoots of the audience.

"Nobody said there'd be clowns!" yelled a voice.

"An added attraction!" the president improvised. "Some innocent buffoonery to provide a respite from the savagery of steel."

He stepped briskly over to the struggling combatants and pinned Donal's right arm under his foot. Bending down, he pulled the dagger from the pirate's grasp. "Get off the stage," he told them in a low voice, "and settle your drunken brawl somewhere else."

Donal aimed an angry kick at the president, giving Will the chance to punch his opponent in the ear and hold him down. The pirate elbowed his way free and lashed out with both fists while Will paid him back, blow for blow.

Suddenly a colossal roar from the crowd made them freeze in mid-punch. They looked up to see Walter and Grace come crashing through one of the stage doors in a flurry of flashing steel. They circled each other in a whirlwind dance, feinting, stabbing and parrying.

"Look at that garb! That's the Italian!" someone cried.

"Begad, he's a woman!" exclaimed another.

"Even so, I'll wager four shillings on her! She's a tiger's heart under that woman's hide!"

"My money's on the other! He'll tame the wildcat!"

Yells of encouragement rang out for both fencers and gamblers barked out their wagers. Walter's advantage in size and strength was matched by Grace's speed and it seemed neither could land a decisive blow on the other.

"This Amazon princess spent five years as a prisoner in the harem of the Turkish Sultan before escaping to ply her trade with the sword," the president informed his delighted audience. "This strapping fellow is the youngest son of the King of Navarre, who once held the gates of Agragassa single-handed against a thousand bloodthirsty Moors."

Fingers clawing viciously at his throat brought Will's attention back to his own fight. He twisted about and butted his knee into Donal's chin. The pirate grabbed his leg and wrestled him over on to his back. Pummelling each other with fists, knees and elbows, they rolled across the stage towards the fencers.

Grace made a quick side-step to avoid them. That moment's distraction was all the chance Walter needed.

Slipping past her guard, he scored a bloody gash across her sword arm. Grace uttered a violent curse as the blade dropped from her fingers and she fell back, clutching her wound.

"A hit, a palpable hit!" announced the president. "Victory to the young prince!"

The spectators stamped their feet, clapping and cheering in a frenzy of excitement. In the heat of the moment, Walter turned unthinkingly to acknowledge the applause with an airy wave of his hand.

At that moment Donal broke loose of Will's grasp and surged to his feet. He launched himself at Walter like a battering ram, striking him solidly in the back. Both men shot off the edge of the stage and plunged headlong into the cheering throng. They disappeared among the sweaty bodies like they had been sucked into a whirlpool.

Grace grabbed her sword and ran off through the stage door. Groaning, Will clambered to his feet and raced after her, his body aching from the beating he had taken. He ran through the tiring house and out the back door. Grace was only a few yards away, sagging against the wall. Her sword was sheathed and her teeth were gritted against the pain of her bleeding arm.

All at once Will saw not a dangerous pirate queen, but

simply an injured woman. Pulling out a kerchief he went to her aid.

"Here, let me bandage that," he said.

Grace tensed at his approach, then smiled crookedly through her pain when she saw he was trying to help.

"So you're still dogging my heels, eh, Will?" she said as he tied his kerchief round the wound. "It must be love for sure. You'll be writing me poems next."

"It's only Christian to help somebody who's hurt," Will said stiffly, "even if it's an enemy."

"Well, you're a fair foe to be sure," said Grace.

"I don't think you're the ruthless creature Walter says Grace O'Malley is either," said Will.

Grace gave a soft laugh. "Those tales have a way of growing. But don't put my mercy to the test, Will. Be off with you."

They both started at a sudden rumble of wheels and the snorting of two black horses being reined in. A coach richly emblazoned with the coat of arms of the Spanish crown pulled up in front of them. Two men jumped off the back, grabbed hold of Will and bundled him inside. He was pressed into a seat opposite the Spanish ambassador Mendoza, who produced a pistol from beneath his cloak. As his men climbed back aboard the ambassador leaned out of his window to address Grace.

"Signora O'Malley, I see that this boy is one of your crew. If you want him to live, bring the book to my house and we will complete our business on my terms."

The driver set a whip to the horses and the coach lurched off. As they raced down the road to London, the ambassador settled back in his seat and adjusted the points on his lace collar. He eyed Will with a thin smile and pointed the pistol at his heart.

"My king pays a bag of silver for every English pirate slain," he said. "You had best pray your lady captain sets a higher price on your life than that."

20

A Prisoner of Spain

The carriage rumbled through the Bishop's Gate and on into the City. Will weighed the notion of jumping out, but he knew he would not be quick enough to dodge a bullet.

Mendoza appeared to read his mind. "Do not think to escape," he said. "You are a pirate after all, and if I shoot you, I have only to say you forced your way into my carriage to rob me."

Will looked at the pistol and the firm grip the ambassador held on it. For all his fine clothes, he had the air of a military man and Will had no doubt he was a deadly shot.

"Tell me your name," said Mendoza, "so if the worst should happen I can see you decently buried."

Will considered telling the whole truth, but promptly abandoned the idea. It would be signing his own death warrant to tell Mendoza that he was working with Walter Raleigh to recover the *Meta Incognita* and keep it out of the Spaniard's hands. Right now all that was keeping him alive was the ambassador's belief that he could use him as a bargaining chip with Grace O'Malley.

"My name… " he said, wondering what would be a good name for a pirate. "Robin's my name, Robin Goodfellow."

"Good fellow," said Mendoza, amused. "Your English names are very quaint."

"You'd best not do me any harm," Will warned. "The captain has a dreadful fondness for vengeance."

Mendoza raised a sardonic eyebrow. "Oh really?"

"Yes," said Will grimly. "She once killed a man, his wife, all five of his children and two of his cousins, all because he kicked the ship's cat."

"Yes, I am sure she is very formidable," said Mendoza unconcernedly. "So tell me, Master Goodfellow, how did one so young and mild of appearance come to be part of this bloodthirsty crew?"

Will ransacked his brain, pulling together scraps from the

many stories he had heard and read. "I'm an orphan," he said. "My parents were killed when lightning struck the roof of our church one dark Sunday and brought it crashing down on the heads of half the parish. Forced to make my own way in the world, I travelled on foot to Portsmouth and signed on as a cabin boy aboard an honest merchant vessel."

"That is very enterprising of you," Mendoza complimented him.

"Well, we set out on a dangerous voyage far across the Atlantic," Will continued, "and three weeks out we sailed into the blackest storm that ever darkened the sky. The wind ripped away our sails and the waves cracked our hull like it was a nut. The ship was wrecked and only I survived to be washed ashore on an unknown island in the far west."

"Surely God has blessed you with a special care," said Mendoza, drawing a cross in the air with the barrel of his pistol.

"Yes, I thank God for preserving me," said Will, crossing himself. "I lived by hunting wild beasts with a spear I made from a tree branch and a sharpened piece of shell. One day a pirate vessel landed there to take on fresh water. They offered me the chance to be one of their crew or be left in lonely isolation for the rest of my days. I decided that human company, of whatever sort, was the better choice, so I joined them and bound myself to the captain with such oaths as it would freeze your blood to hear."

Mendoza set his pistol down and clapped. "Storms, shipwreck and wild beasts!" he laughed. "That's a tale to match the romances of Boccaccio and Ariosto."

"Stranger things happen every day than what you read about in books," said Will feelingly. He was beginning to learn just how true that was.

"Well, if God still has a care for you," said the ambassador, picking up his gun again, "he will send your captain promptly to trade for you. If not, you will wish you had stayed on your island."

They drew up in the walled courtyard of a large house. A servant opened the carriage door and Mendoza sent Will out ahead of him. He was led into the house by the two men who had snatched him and pushed into a chair in a reception room. One of them stood over him while the other left to attend to the ambassador.

The room was lavishly carpeted and there was a small bookcase with about two dozen volumes stored in it. To Will's left hung a large, bloody crucifix and on the opposite wall was a huge painting of a sea battle with cannon blazing and ships on fire.

As the sky outside grew dark, he was surprised by the arrival of a servant, who brought him a tray of food and a tankard of beer. Will gratefully devoured the spiced chicken and crusty bread. He was finishing up the scraps when Mendoza entered the room and sat down on the other side of the table.

"Did you enjoy the meal?" the ambassador asked. "I have my own cook I brought with me from Spain."

"Yes, it was good," said Will. "Thank you."

The ambassador nodded. "I would not want it on my conscience that I sent a man to his death on an empty stomach."

His voice bristled with such cold threat that Will felt his meal coming back on him. Forcing it down, he said, "I'm sure it won't come to that."

"You do not sound confident," said Mendoza, "and I do not blame you. Signora O'Malley has not appeared and my patience is almost done. It seems there is very little of what is called honour among thieves."

"A pirate crew's different," Will improvised. "We swear oaths and things. In blood."

"Yes, a pirate's oath," sneered Mendoza. "If Signora O'Malley had kept her bargain with me, you would not be here now, enjoying your last meal." He paused to smile at Will while his words sank in. "But if you do not wish to entrust your life to a pirate's honesty, you have another option."

"What's that?" asked Will, sensing a trap.

Mendoza leaned over the table. "You could take my part in this. If you tell me where Signora O'Malley is hiding, then I can go fetch the book for myself. Not only would you live, but you would find yourself richly rewarded." He chuckled softly. "You would have enough money to go home and repair the roof of your church."

Will's heart sank. If he revealed that he didn't have the information the Spaniard wanted, he might be killed right now. "Wouldn't that make me a sort of traitor?" he asked.

Mendoza stood up and glowered down at him. "A traitor to whom? To your pirate captain? If she were in your place she would take the money like that." He snapped his fingers. "To your heretic queen? Her own country seethes with rebellion against her and she will soon be embroiled in a ruinous war with France. It is only a matter of time before my king sends his ships to sweep her from the throne."

He came and stood directly over Will. "Until now I have been a genial host," he said, "but you have not much time left."

He nodded to the guard who drew his sword and ran a finger down the blade.

Will bowed his head and tried desperately to think of some way out. Mendoza had dismissed his story of the desert island as a boy's fanciful invention, harmless and amusing, but the next lie he told might be the one that killed him. He had to invent something that would give the Spaniard pause before his frustration drove him to do away with his prisoner.

Like a shaft of sunlight breaking through the clouds, an idea came to Will, so audacious he was almost afraid to use it. But perhaps, if he could act the part well enough, it might buy him some time. He looked up and met Mendoza's gaze with an unflinching eye.

"I don't know what's delaying her," he said, "but you can be sure Grace O'Malley will come for me."

The ambassador regarded him curiously, impressed by his confident tone. "Tell me why I should be so sure," he said.

Will kept his voice firm as a rock as he took his gamble. "Because I'm her son."

21

The Reluctant Pirate

"Her son?" Mendoza repeated dubiously.

"Why else would she keep me around?" asked Will. "You said yourself I'm not much of a pirate."

Mendoza stepped back and scrutinised his captive, searching for some trace of deception. "You said you were an orphan."

"I didn't want you to know the truth," said Will. "That's why I made up that stupid story." He let his shoulders slump and shook his head. "To tell you the truth, I hate being at sea. I'm sick half the time and she expects me to do twice as much work as the rest of the crew. She says it will make a man of me."

He let some pain leak into his voice and even managed to squeeze one small tear from his left eye to complete the effect. Mendoza stroked his chin and signalled his man to sheath his sword. He paced the room, darting quick glances back at Will, as if trying to catch him out. Will continued to look beaten and dejected.

Mendoza stopped in front of him at last. "If you are telling the truth," he said with the beginnings of a smile, "then I may demand all that I want of her."

There was a tap at the door and a servant entered. He spoke to the ambassador in Spanish and Mendoza's smile widened into a wolfish grin. "Now we'll settle the matter, my reluctant pirate," he said. "Your mother is here to ransom you."

The news hit Will like a dash of cold water to the face. He had concocted his daring lie when he'd given up all hope of Grace showing up. Now he realised he had probably doubled his peril.

The door opened and Grace came in with two armed Spaniards at her back. She was still dressed in a man's garb with a hooded cloak wrapped round her shoulders. As she entered the room she threw back the hood and shook out her long, black hair.

The ambassador made a small bow. "Signora O'Malley,

how kind of you to accept my invitation."

"I'm here to conclude our business," Grace retorted bluntly. "Don't dress it up in ribbons."

She took a leather satchel from under her arm and laid it on the table. "I'll have my gold now," she said.

"And what about this fine-looking young man?" Mendoza asked. "Surely you want him too."

"I'll take him along to carry the gold," Grace said, barely glancing at Will.

"I think he is worth much more to you than any amount of gold," said Mendoza.

Grace gave him a curious squint. "I didn't come here to crack riddles with you, Signor," she said. "All the use he is to me is to scrub the decks and empty the slops, and he does a poor enough job of that."

Mendoza laughed. "I do not fault you for trying to keep the secret, but the boy has already told me the truth."

Grace looked suspiciously from Will to Mendoza. "What secret? What truth?"

"There's no use pretending any more," Will told her. "He knows the whole truth, *mother*."

Grace stared at him as if he had just grown horns.

"Take your son," said Mendoza, "and let his good treatment at my hands stand in place of money."

Grace curled her lip. "Him? My son?"

The contempt in her voice pricked Will like a needle. She sauntered over to where he was seated and cupped his chin in her hand. "Look at him!" she said, tilting his head back. "There's more milk and cakes in him than steel and salt water. He's no more an O'Malley than you're a Viking."

"But you came for him," said Mendoza, confused.

Grace let Will's chin drop and stepped away from him. "I came for my payment," she insisted. "As for this poor fool, you'd be as well to lock him away in Bedlam with the rest of the lunatics."

"Lunatics?" Mendoza echoed.

"Yes, lunatics," said Grace, turning her back on Will and retracing her steps to where the satchel lay. "Don't you have madmen in Spain? One day he claims to be a king's son, next he's a fairy child captured by a magician. Oh, he's a sore trial to me!"

Will swallowed hard and listened in anxious silence. Once again it seemed that Grace was going to humiliate him and leave.

Mendoza considered briefly, then waved a dismissive hand. "In my work I have enough deceit to untangle without inviting more," he said. "Take him and be a mother or murderer to him, as you wish."

Will rose and made his way cautiously to Grace's side, fearing that at any moment the Spaniard might change his mind.

"Ah Will," said Grace, ruffling his hair, "are you not ashamed to be lying to this fine gentleman?" Then she gave him a clip across the back of the head and added sharply, "I'll put up with no more of your tales, mind. From now on you're to be a good and honest boy."

Will hung his head and looked suitably ashamed. "I'll try," he muttered. He was willing to play any part now as long as it would get them clear of this house.

"Now, Signor, my money," said Grace, extending her hand, "and we'll part as friends. Maybe we can even do business again another day."

"Not so hasty, Signora O'Malley," said Mendoza, raising a chiding finger. "I will not be a man who pays for a pearl then finds the oyster empty."

He unbuckled the satchel Grace had brought and slid out the green book. He frowned. "There is a lock on it. Have you not looked inside?"

"I thought you'd want the goods undamaged," said Grace. "You can examine it at your leisure, but I've the tide to catch if I'm to get away to Ireland before the English agents catch up with me."

Something in her tone told Will she was acting and that she had managed to unlock the book. In which case, why did she want to get away before Mendoza read it?

"Is there a not a saying in this country," said the ambassador, "that a book should not be judged by its cover?" He tapped the book with his finger. "Juan!" he said, summoning forward the largest of his guards, a huge man with only one ear.

At a command from his master, the guard drew his dagger and stabbed it into the leather cover. He prised the brass lock loose, then ripped it away. The job done he backed off, leaving the ambassador to examine his prize.

Will saw Grace edge towards the door, but at a word from Mendoza the guards blocked her way. The ambassador turned page after page, flipping them faster and faster in mounting anger.

He rounded furiously on Grace and barked an order at his men. Two guards seized her by the arms and one of them wrenched her sword and dagger from her belt, tossing them to the floor.

"Now I see why you were so eager to be gone," Mendoza accused. He pointed back at the book. "This is a nonsense, a book of tricks and puzzles!"

"It's what you sent me to fetch!" Grace answered with

equal fury. "Don't blame me if it's not written in Spanish!"

"It is not written in any language!" Mendoza retorted. "Did you think to fool me with this while you keep the true *Meta Incognita* for yourself?"

"This is it!" Grace insisted. "I took it from its hiding place with my own hands."

"Then your hands are as perjured as your tongue!" roared Mendoza.

While they quarrelled, Will inched closer to the book to examine it for himself. Turning the pages, he saw meaningless strings of letters alternating with rows of random numbers, weird symbols set in elaborate grids, dots, lines and numerals scattered about in no discernible order.

Mendoza shoved him aside and slammed the book shut. "I give you one hour to reconsider your treachery," he told Grace, "or to make your peace with God. After that, a quick death is the only mercy you can expect of me."

He gave a curt order to his men and the big guard seized hold of Will. He and Grace were dragged out of the room and down a flight of stairs to a gloomy dungeon.

22

A Hare in a Maze

"You gutless ratspawn!" Grace yelled back at Mendoza. "A hell of blazing poxes on you, your king – and your *horse*!"

Struggling and spitting, she was thrown into a dimly lit cell. Will was bundled roughly inside after her. The guards had no sooner finished locking the door than Grace was kicking it in a frenzy of temper.

"You whoreson, godless dogs!" she raged. "You dung-stuffed, bog-supping lackwits! You cankerous puttocks!"

She carried on in an ecstasy of obscenity, hurling wave upon wave of shocking profanity at the Spaniards. Will had heard his father swear on occasion but this was something else entirely. Grace made the most foul-mouthed drunk in Stratford sound like a nun at prayer. Will was half afraid God would obliterate the entire house with a thunderbolt just to shut her up.

Much to his relief she eventually gave the door a final kick and broke off her rant. She took a deep breath, as if she had just completed a five mile run. "That'll curdle their ears, sure enough!" she declared with some satisfaction.

"It's not done a lot for my health either," Will complained.

Grace clapped him on the shoulder. "It's just words, Will, not bullets. You'll live a mite longer yet."

Will wasn't so sure. Nor was he sure that Grace O'Malley was the best company to die in. He doubted any angels would come within ten miles of them after her blasphemous tirade, and that left only one other place for their souls to go.

He squatted down on the floor and contemplated their miserable situation. A horrible thought occurred to him. "You don't suppose they'll torture us before they kill us, do you?"

Grace leaned against the wall and hooked her thumbs into her belt. "I've given birth to four strapping children," she said. "One aboard a ship being chased by Barbary pirates. *That's* pain. I'd like to see those fancy-breeches do worse."

"It's all right for you," said Will. "You're used to this kind of thing. You're a pirate."

"Pirate?" said Grace. "You English call me that for sure, but to my own people back in Ireland I'm a leader and protector. When times are hard and the harvest fails, I'm the one who'll fight and steal to see them fed."

"It's not hunger I'm worried about," said Will.

"I warned you to keep clear of me, Will," Grace told him. "You should have listened."

"Walter explained about the book, what's inside it. I had to help him get it back."

"Walter Raleigh?" Grace laughed richly. "Oh, he's a fine looking fellow, I'll grant him that, but he's as much a blockhead as any other man. I live in hope that one day I'll meet a man with half a brain between his ears."

"What will you do then?" Will asked.

"Oh, I'll probably have to kill him," Grace replied with a shrug. "That's the way my luck usually runs."

"Don't you hope," Will began hesitantly, "one day to, maybe, love somebody?"

Grace pushed her hair back from her face and sighed. "There was a lad I loved once, many a long year ago. Hugh was his name. I found him washed up on the shore after a shipwreck."

"That's just the way we found you," said Will. "Though you were only pretending."

Grace slid down the wall until she was sitting on the floor eye to eye with Will. He fell silent before her gaze and let her carry on with her story.

"I nursed him back to health and took him for my lover." Grace's face broke into a smile that seemed to turn her back into a young girl with hardly a care in her heart. "Oh, he had a laugh like bells on Sunday and when he kissed me it was as sweet as fresh spring water."

There was a long silence. Finally Will asked, "What happened to him?"

Grace's smile hardened into ice. "He was out hunting in the hills one day when some enemies of mine came upon him. They murdered him out of sheer spite towards me, even though he never did them any harm."

Her eyes were staring back through time now, as if she could see the grisly scene laid out before her. For a moment Will was reminded of Venus mourning for Adonis.

"I caught up with them," Grace said bitterly. "I tracked down and killed every one of them with my own hands."

She looked sadly at Will. "There. That's the true tale of Grace O'Malley. Now do you think me a monster?"

"You acted out of love," said Will, "for all you did a terrible thing."

"Out of love, yes," said Grace, rubbing her right arm where Raleigh had cut her in the swordfight. "But the worst of it is, no matter how much vengeance you take, it never kills the hurt it grew from." Her shoulders slumped, as if all the heart had been drained out of her. "Well, all my hurts will be over soon," she sighed.

"I had a little sister, Ann," said Will. "She died just this past winter."

Grace stirred from her own memories and gazed at him curiously.

"But sometimes," Will said, "when I look out the window, I think I still see her playing in the garden, picking flowers and counting the petals. Maybe death isn't the end of things after all."

Grace laid a sympathetic hand on his arm. "Will, if I can persuade Mendoza you're a harmless loon, he'll maybe let you go, for it's said God loves a fool."

At the touch of her hand Will felt something stir inside him: the sure certainty that he didn't want either one of them to die. He thought about the *Meta Incognita*, its complexity, the labyrinthine library Grace had stolen it from.

"Look," he said, "you already opened the book and read it, didn't you?"

"I know a man who can pick a lock as easy as you pull on your boots," answered Grace. "But like you saw, it's all written in some infernal code."

"And you've no idea how to translate it?"

Grace spat in the corner and uttered a ripe curse. Will was glad to see a flash of her old fire. "I tried, God knows," she said, "tracing the letters with my finger, trying to catch the sense of it, but every time I think I've nipped it by the tail it escapes me, like a hare dashing down a maze."

"A maze," Will repeated. Something was nagging at him, a memory of the day he first arrived at Mortlake, following Dr Dee past rows and rows of books to the centre of the library. On the table there he saw a book entitled *A True Treatise On The Construction Of The Labyrinth Of King Minos*. It was a book about how to construct a maze – and it was bound in exactly the same green leather as the *Meta Incognita.*

He jumped up excitedly. "We're not done for yet, Grace!" he exclaimed. "I think I can get us out of here!"

23

A Pretty Piece of Thieving

"Yes, I know it is a code!" Mendoza said irritably. "I did not grant you these few minutes of life so you could tell me what I already know."

Will saw Grace's jaw clench tight as she bit back a lashing reply. They had agreed Will would do the talking, then called the guards to take them to Mendoza, offering to confess all.

"Look at it," said Will, flipping the green book open. "There's not one code here but many. It would take years to crack all of them."

"And do you have the keys to the codes in your head?"

Mendoza inquired sharply. "For if not you are wasting valuable time you should be spending in prayer."

"That's the point," said Will. "There are too many. Nobody could possibly memorise them all."

"I do not see how this is good news for you," said Mendoza, waving his guards forward. "You offer me no reason to be merciful."

"Let him finish, you pox-addled fool!" Grace exclaimed.

Mendoza's nostrils flared at the insult.

"The codes are written down in *another* book," Will interjected quickly. "You need both books to understand the text."

Mendoza was intrigued now. "A second book, you say?" He ran his finger over the open page of the *Meta Incognita*. "And where is that to be found?"

"In Dr Dee's library," said Will. "He has thousands of books there."

"If there are so many, how can you pick out the right one?" asked Mendoza.

"I saw it once," said Will. "I'm sure I could find it again."

"Is this another lie?" Mendoza asked, his eyes shifting back and forth between Grace and Will.

"He was at Mortlake with me," said Grace. "I had him

worm his way into Dee's confidence to help me find the *Meta Incognita*."

"I know I can find it," Will insisted. He pointed to the crucifix on the wall. "I'll swear on the cross if you like."

"A pirate's oath!" Mendoza sneered. "You might as well swear on a barrel of rum."

"What other choice do you have?" asked Grace. "Do you want to bring an army up the Thames and lay siege to Mortlake? That would be tipping your hand a mite, wouldn't it?"

Mendoza waved his men back and Grace broke out in a broad grin. "Now you're showing there's some brains under that perfumed mop of yours." She picked up Dee's book and the satchel, tucking them both under her cloak.

"Hold there!" Mendoza exclaimed. "Do you think I am going to let you leave with that?"

Grace placed a hand on her hip and stared at the ambassador as if he was a difficult schoolboy. "And what use is it to you just now?" she asked tartly. "Are you planning to take it to your king so he can beat your brains out with it?"

"No," said Mendoza, "but I would be a fool to let you take it."

"We have to go back to Mortlake and trick the key out of Dr Dee," said Grace. "He won't let us take two steps over his threshold if we don't bring his precious book with us."

Turning away, she stuffed the book back in its satchel and pulled her cloak tightly around her. Mendoza snapped an order at his men who immediately barred her way. Grace whirled about and glowered at him.

"Unless I hold on to the *Meta Incognita*," said the ambassador, "I have no guarantee that you will return. As things stand now, if you bring me the second book, I will pay you all that you are owed."

"And how in the name of the Almighty do you expect us to get in and out of Dee's house unnoticed?" Grace asked.

Mendoza stroked his moustache thoughtfully, as if coming to a difficult decision. "I tell you this in confidence," he said. "There are revels planned at Mortlake tomorrow night. I know for a fact that events will take an unexpected turn, so much so that you will have all the distraction you need to enter and depart unseen. The rest I leave to your resourcefulness."

Will held his breath, praying silently that Grace's temper wouldn't trip them up at this last hurdle. She appeared to ponder a moment then strode over to the table and laid down the satchel.

"I'll need my weapons back if we're to fight our way out of Mortlake," she told the ambassador.

Mendoza gave instruction to one of his men who fetched Grace's sword and dagger and handed them over to her. Sheathing the weapons she turned to Will. "Come on, Will, let's be off."

The Spanish guards escorted them down the hallway, stopping at the front door to watch them make their way across the courtyard. Will felt as if he were crossing a bridge made of twigs that might collapse at any second. In the night sky above the half moon looked as if it were turning its face away from the knavish tricks of mortals.

"Devil take him for not trusting me!" Grace muttered under her breath.

Her words jogged Will's memory. With all their efforts to escape Mendoza's house he had not thought to ask her about the Devil's Fire. "Grace," he said, "you have to tell me about the Dev—"

"Hush and walk faster, Will!" Grace cut him off.

Will's stomach sank. "Why?"

"I've got the book pinned under my arm. It was my gloves I stuffed in the bag. A pretty piece of thieving, don't you think?"

"Very pretty," Will groaned. "But we won't be if Mendoza gets his hands on us."

At that moment an angry cry exploded inside the house like a gunshot. The ambassador had opened the satchel.

"Abandon ship, Will!" Grace cried, breaking into a run.

Will raced after her out into the dark street. He bumped into her back as she swerved into an alley and pulled up short. Donal was waiting there for her.

"You had me worried, Grace!" said Donal. "You were gone that long."

"Negotiations turned a mite thorny," Grace told him. She peered down the alley and let out an angry hiss. "What's this?"

"We found this peacock sneaking up on the Signor's house, so we bagged him for you," said Donal proudly.

A few yards down the alley stood two more pirates holding Walter prisoner between them. One had taken his sword while the other held a knife to his throat.

"Walter Raleigh, I've had husbands that didn't stick as close as you do!" Grace exclaimed in disgust. "Is there no way to shake loose of you?"

"I promise you'll have none of my company when you're locked in the Tower," said Walter. He looked curiously at Will. "I searched for you, Will, but there was no trace. How did you get here?"

Before Will could reply there came a clatter of boot heels

from the street and a band of armed Spaniards charged into view.

"Let him go, boys!" Grace ordered abruptly. "We've bigger trouble on our hands!"

At least half a dozen Spaniards poured into the alley. The first was carrying a heavy musket, which he braced against his shoulder ready to fire.

Quick as the snap of a whip, Grace swept her sword from its sheath and swung it at full stretch to dash the gun barrel aside. The shot boomed through the alley like a thunderclap and the powder flash dazzled Spaniards and pirates alike. The bullet missed its target and split open a rain barrel with a sharp crack.

As everyone reeled from the sudden flare, Will saw Grace had dropped the *Meta Incognita*. Coughing from the musket smoke, he made a lunge and scooped it up. As the Spaniards surged forward, Walter reclaimed his sword and leapt to meet them.

"Get away, Will!" he ordered as the pirates formed up around him and Grace. "Head for the river!"

Will tried to break away, but the fight was all around him now. Every step he took he was jostled or tripped by the furious combatants. The alley echoed with the clang of steel and a dinning chorus of threats and curses. Grace and

Walter fought back to back now, too caught up in the battle even to insult each other.

Falling to his knees, Will wormed his way through a thicket of stamping legs. Once clear, he sprang to his feet again. Tucking the book under his arm, he pelted down the alley and round the corner into a small open court.

Head for the river, Walter had said. But which way was it?

As he tried to take his bearings, the sound of running feet made him turn to face another Spaniard with a musket. The man levelled the gun at him. "Stand where you are!" he ordered.

Will froze in panic. Smiling grimly, the Spaniard adjusted his aim and touched his finger to the trigger.

24

Shooting the Bridge

Will had a desperate flash of inspiration. Whipping the book out from under his arm, he placed it square across his chest. Relief almost made him giddy when the Spaniard lowered his gun and snarled in frustration.

He had guessed rightly that Mendoza's men had orders to retrieve the book and none of them dared risk blasting a hole through it. The Spaniard advanced on him and Will backed away. Glancing behind him he saw a narrow street that bent sharply after a few yards, but if he turned to make a dash for it, he wouldn't be able to use the book as a shield.

Suddenly a tumult erupted behind the Spaniard who

whirled round to see two of his fellows spill into the square, locked in combat with Donal and one of his shipmates. Seizing his chance, Will spun about and raced off down the narrow street. The Spaniard shouted and raised his musket.

The bang of exploding powder smacked the air and the street lit up as if hit by lightning. Will felt a hot gust at his cheek as the bullet whistled past and cracked the plaster of a nearby building.

The shock spurred him on and he raced for the end of the lane, wheeling round the corner. He ran for his life, bumping off walls and skidding on the refuse that lay scattered over the cobbles.

Another musket shot boomed out somewhere close by and Will bolted in the opposite direction. Down this street then left up another. He was running so fast he was only dimly aware of dashing out on to an embankment. He reeled to a stop on the very edge of the walk with the grey water of the Thames lapping twenty feet below him. As he tottered on the brink, he was grabbed by the collar and hauled back to safety.

"The Thames is no place to go swimming, Will," joked Raleigh "You wouldn't believe some of the things people toss in there."

"Walter!" Will exclaimed in relief. "How did you know to find me at the ambassador's?"

"Well, after a couple of hours searching for you, I decided the best thing I could do was track down Grace O'Malley," Walter explained. "The best way to do that was to keep an eye on Mendoza's house, but I'd no sooner got there than those pirates ambushed me." Smiling, he took the book from Will and patted the cover. "Still, all's well that ends well, eh?" Another clash of swords echoed through the buildings behind them. "Time to go!"

Towing Will after him, Raleigh set out along the embankment. A hundred yards upriver they came to a flight of steps leading down to a stone jetty. Here, seated in a rowing boat and preparing to cast off, was Lok, the man from the icy north.

"Best speed, Lok, best speed!" Walter urged as he and Will climbed aboard.

"Speed?" said Lok. "I am almost asleep waiting for you to come back."

He set his powerful shoulders to the oars and pulled away from the bank. Will looked out across the river and saw a few barges drifting along as well as a scattering of other rowing boats ferrying late night revellers back home. Most of the boats carried lanterns and many of the passengers were singing to each other.

A rapid drumming of running feet caused him to turn

back towards the bank. "Look!" he exclaimed, pointing.

Walter looked and groaned as Grace O'Malley came pelting down the steps towards them. "Hold up there!" she yelled, sheathing her sword.

Walter clapped Lok on the shoulder. "Go! Go! She can swim if she needs to."

Putting on a final burst of speed, Grace ran full tilt down the jetty and took a flying leap off the end, her cloak billowing about her. She crashed into their midst, burying Walter beneath her. The boat lurched perilously to one side.

"Have a care!" Lok cried. "You'll overturn us!"

Dropping the oars he seized hold of the pirate queen and dragged her off his companion. "You she-devil!" gasped Walter. "Are you trying to sink us?"

Grace righted herself with a toss of her head. "Leave off your griping, Walter! Surely you didn't mean to leave me to Signor Mendoza's harsh mercies. That wouldn't be gentlemanly."

"It's you that got us into all of this," Will accused her. "It's a lucky thing any of us are alive."

Grace gave him a look of feigned disappointment. "Oh, Will, and there was I thinking you were one of my crew now."

"Enough talk!" Lok rumbled. "See what is coming!"

They all stared and Will swallowed hard. A long, sleek boat rowed by six Spaniards was pulling away from another jetty. It swung round on its keel and came driving towards them with gathering speed. Mendoza stood in the prow, urging his men on with a wave of his pistol.

"He has his own barge!" groaned Walter. He dropped the book and took one of the oars from Lok. "Row for it!" he urged. "We've got to keep clear of them!"

The two men pulled mightily, rowing downriver for all they were worth.

Straightening his arm, Mendoza braced himself against the motion of the boat and took careful aim with his pistol.

Grace slapped Walter on the knee. "Put your back into it, man! He's a dead shot, so I hear."

"If you're not happy, why don't you take the oar?" Walter grunted.

Grace clutched her wounded arm and grimaced. "Don't think I wouldn't if you hadn't cut my arm, you miserable son of a sea cook!"

A plume of smoke belched from Mendoza's gun. The bullet punched a hole in one of the boat's wooden ribs, puncturing it only inches above the water line.

Grace blew the ambassador a mocking kiss and called out, "Bad luck, Signor!"

"If I could spare a moment I'd toss you in the water and let him have you," Walter growled.

Grace tilted her head coquettishly. "Walter, if you keep talking like that, I'll be thinking you're not in love with me any more."

"In love!" Walter exclaimed through gritted teeth. He tried to come up with a suitably outraged rebuttal, but words failed him. Instead he threw all his energy into the oar.

Lok was rowing so furiously the bones on his necklace were rattling. Both men were red-faced and sweating. Lok squinted at their pursuers. "They are catching us."

"They row like Argonauts, damn them!" said Walter.

"And there's the Bridge, dead ahead!" Will warned.

The dark bulk of London Bridge loomed before them, only a few pale lights dotted among its windows. Once they fetched up against it the Spaniards would have them.

"We're between a rock and a whirlpool, and that's a fact," Grace declared ruefully.

"Can we make it to the bank?" Walter asked his companion.

Lok shook his head. "They would be on us too quick. There is one chance, if you have the stomach for it."

"The stomach for what?" Will asked uneasily.

"To shoot the Bridge," Lok replied grimly.

"You mean go under?" exclaimed Walter. "Nobody goes under London Bridge. The channels between the pillars are too narrow. The current would wreck us."

"I knew a man who tried it," said Lok. "His passengers were drunk but rich and paid him well to dare it."

"So what happened to the brave fellow?" asked Grace.

"The boat was smashed to pieces and all of them drowned," Lok answered.

"God's nails, man!" Walter gasped. "What makes you think you can succeed?"

"I will say a prayer to my goddess Sedna," Lok said, as if that settled the matter.

"Well, that's a comfort!" said Grace, slumping back in the stern. "He's got a goddess to help him."

"We've no choice," said Walter, tight-lipped. "I hope this Sedna loves you, Lok."

"I am a fine, handsome man," Lok assured him. "Sedna loves me very much."

Will picked up the *Meta Incognita* from where Walter had dropped it. "We need something to protect the book," he said. "You know, just in case…"

"There is a cape of sealskin under the seat below you," said Lok. "I keep it against the rain."

Will pulled out the sealskin and wrapped it tightly around the book.

"Here, Will, let me take care of that for you," said Grace, stretching out a hand. "It's brought you enough trouble already."

"No, I don't think so," said Will, stuffing it deep inside his shirt.

Lok and Walter steered for the nearest opening under the Bridge. Will saw that the Spaniards had guessed what they were up to and had redoubled their efforts, urged on by Mendoza's angry cries. If Lok and Walter slowed even a fraction they'd be caught. Ahead of them lay escape – or death.

"Here it comes," said Walter. "Hold on!"

The gap yawned before them like a hungry maw. Lok and Walter dragged their oars into the boat as Grace and Will gripped the hull. With a sickening lurch the rabid current seized hold and shot them into the blackness.

25

Proof Positive

It was like diving headlong down the throat of a colossal sea beast. The roar of the water echoed deafeningly off the walls of the tunnel and the massive weight of the bridge overhead pressed down on them like the crushing hand of a stone giant. Above the tumult Will could hear Lok's keening voice singing out to Sedna, the goddess of the frozen North.

Whether it was Lok's skill that saved them, the blessing of his goddess or sheer luck Will didn't know, but the next moment they came flying out under the stars, propelled across the water by the sheer momentum of the current.

"By the Virgin, we made it!" cried Grace.

They all let out a triumphant whoop that was cut short by the sight of what lay dead ahead. Walter and Lok made a scramble for the oars, but it was too late to turn.

Twenty yards beyond the Bridge floated a merchant galley surrounded by boatloads of English soldiers and customs officers. Some of them waved their arms and shouted futile warnings as they saw the rowing boat shoot out from under the bridge and come flying straight at them like an arrow from a bow.

Lok's boat struck head on. The prow cracked open and the stern bounced into the air, pitching all four passengers into the river. The impact knocked Will senseless as he plunged into the water. Down and down he sank into a cold, black nothingness. As his senses returned he realised he couldn't tell up from down and he began to panic.

He had instinctively taken a breath when he was slammed out of the boat but he hadn't much air left. Kicking vigorously, he fought the powerful tug of the current and struck out for the surface. Stubbornly he worked his way upwards stroke by stroke.

A rough rash of barnacles grazed his knuckles. To his horror he realised the tide had swept him right under the ship. His lungs were on fire, his chest a knot of agony. Trapped inside his shirt, Dee's book dragged on him like an anchor. Clawing at the hull, he followed the upward curve of the ship's side. Then, just as the last of his strength was giving out, his head broke the surface.

Will's first gulp of air was like a draught from Heaven. But before he could take another he was ploughed down by an oncoming rowboat. Water forced its way into his open mouth and down his throat. Even as he gave himself up for lost, he was lifted up on the sweep of an oar.

"Heave there, neighbour Dulworth!" came a voice.

Two pairs of hands caught hold of Will's jerkin and legs and hauled him up. Powerless to help himself, he was dragged bruisingly over the side to topple into the boat. His chest and stomach knotted convulsively. The next moment he spewed up a bellyful of river water.

"Keep clear of that, neighbour Dulworth!" one of the men warned the other. "You don't want none of that on you."

When he had finished retching and had sucked in three good lungfuls of fresh air, Will finally looked up. Through blurred vision he saw two men standing over him dressed in frayed green tabards that marked them out as constables. One was a lean, scarecrow-like figure with a large, carrot-shaped nose. The other was plump with a round, owlish face. Will tried to thank them but all that came out was a wordless croak.

"What's that he says, neighbour Bellows?" the chubby constable asked.

"Something in his own foreign tongue no doubt," Bellows answered with a knowledgeable air. "You can see to look at him he's no Englishman."

"I – am – English," Will managed to force out.

"Then double the shame upon you for being a smuggler," Bellows scolded.

"An honest Englishman should pay the customs duty that's owed the crown," the round-faced Dulworth added pompously.

Will propped himself up on his elbow and gazed out over the river. There was the ship, the deck crawling with armed men, prisoners being passed down to the boats where constables waited to guard them. He saw no sign of his three companions.

"I'm no smuggler," he protested hoarsely. "My boat was capsized by accident."

"I'm pleased to believe you did not mean to drown," said Bellows, "but you are a smuggler and the proof is as follows. First, that you are neither constable nor soldier. Second, that you are not a fish. In conclusion, you are a smuggler."

"Spoken like a philosophist," the other man complimented him. "There's no trickery can defeat sound argument."

Will shivered and coughed. He felt as if the cold water had seeped right into his bones and he could barely keep his eyes open.

"He's got something hidden under his clothes, neighbour Bellows," Dulworth pointed out.

"You have the right of it, partner," said Bellows. "Let's have a look there, lad. We'll make a proper examination of the matter."

Dulworth held Will in place while Bellows reached into his shirt and dragged the book out.

"What's this then?" Bellows wondered, cocking an eyebrow. "Maybe it's a volume of bawdy pictures from Italy, eh?" He winked at his friend and they both stifled their laughter.

"It's no good to you," said Will, making a grab for the book.

"I'll thank you to keep to your place, my young knave," said Bellows, lofting the book out of his reach. He opened it with a supercilious expression that reminded Will of a schoolmaster. As he turned the pages the constable's expression quickly changed to puzzlement then to horror.

"What's amiss, neighbour Bellows?" Dulworth asked. "You look like you've just caught your wife kissing the butcher's boy." He let out a gurgling laugh that withered away when his companion grabbed the front of his jerkin.

"You won't be laughing when you take a look at this," Bellows informed him curtly. He pulled the other constable's face close to the book and flipped the pages under his nose.

Dulworth screwed up his eyes. "I can't make anything of it, neighbour. Is it Russian?"

Bellows clapped the book shut and smacked his companion over the head with it. "No, it's not Russian, you noddy! This is the devil's alphabet!"

Both men turned on Will with wary suspicion in their eyes.

"It's just a book," Will said weakly.

"No Christian ever wrote such a book," said Bellows, stabbing a finger at the *Meta Incognita*. "And the proof is this. First, it is not Scripture. Second, not being Scripture, it is not holy. In conclusion, as it is unholy, it is the devil's work."

"Most soundly disputed, neighbour," said Dulworth.

Bellows brandished the book like a club. "Magic spells is what this is," he said. "Witch's curses to sink ships and blight cattle."

"A neighbour of mine's best mare was lamed by a witch," Dulworth piped up.

Will tried to sit up but he was too weak. "Horses just go lame," he said. "It's nothing to do with witches."

"And how would you know about that mare," Bellows asked darkly, "unless you had some hand in the cursing?"

"Neighbour Bellows!" Dulworth exclaimed excitedly. "Did you note how he floated on the water like he was made of wood? That's the sure mark of a witch or I'm a blockhead."

"You're right, neighbour, most egregiously right," Bellows agreed. "It is a manifest evidence of witchcraft."

Will's head was so clouded he could almost suppose he was dreaming. "I was just in a boat," he began weakly, trying to muster some defence.

Bellows clamped a sweaty hand over Will's lips. "Neighbour, we'll stop up his mouth before he lays a curse on us!"

They held the prisoner down and silenced him with a gag, then lashed his wrists behind his back with a strip of leather. Once he was secured, the two constables stood over him and nodded in satisfaction.

"Should we take him to the Fleet Prison with the other smugglers?" Dulworth asked.

"No, neighbour Dulworth," Bellows answered with a solemn shake of the head. "The Fleet's for your common, everyday rogues and cutpurses. No, this one's for the Tower."

26

The Protector of England

"Come on, wake up! You've had your sleep!"

Will felt the toe of a boot thump into his ribs.

He moaned groggily as his wrists were untied and the gag wrenched from his mouth. Above him a lantern burned with a sullen, red flame that cast a lurid glow over the cell, but after hours of darkness even this cheerless light was enough to make his eyes smart.

A small grille was set in the ceiling overhead, designed in such a way that it admitted air from outside but no glimmer of light. He was lying on a cold stone floor, over which a handful of dirty straw had been thrown as a meagre covering. Two men stood over him, their faces shadowy in the dim light.

"Off with you now," ordered the nearer of the men as he set his lantern down on a shelf in the wall. "I'll summon you if there's a need."

Will saw the guard who had locked him in here depart, heard his boot heels scuffing on the steps outside. Now he was alone in the cell with a stranger who pulled the door shut and turned to face him.

Will tried to gather his scattered thoughts. He had only a vague recollection of being lifted half-conscious from the constables' boat on to a dock. He was dragged, stumbling, across the grounds of the Tower of London, through a door and down a steep stairway. At the bottom he was flung into a windowless cell like a discarded cloak and left there, bound and gagged.

A pair of snake-like eyes peered at him out of a gaunt, parchment face. The head tilted to one side on a neck that was two inches too long and the thin lips spoke.

"Here, sit on this." The voice was grey and sharp-edged like a broken piece of flint.

The stranger picked up a stool and set it down directly in the centre of the cell. He was dressed in plain black clothes with no lace or finery about him. His sparse yellow hair was heavily oiled and plastered to his skull, his beard no more than a fringe clinging to his chin.

He stood by patiently while Will struggled on to his knees and crawled towards the stool. As soon as he leaned on it, it toppled over and he fell flat on his face, his cheek scraping over the coarse flagstones.

The man in black made no move to help, but watched impassively as Will righted the stool and clambered stiffly on to it. He walked in a full circle round him then stopped in front of the prisoner, his arms folded behind his back.

"Tell me what your name is, my young master."

Will's brow furrowed. He had used so many names already – Shakespeare, Shakeshaft, Goodfellow – he hardly knew which to choose.

"Will," he said. "That's all."

"True or not, it will serve," said the gaunt man, shrugging one slender shoulder.

Will wrapped his arms about himself and tried to stop shivering. His clothes were still dank from being soaked in the Thames, his mouth was parched and rancid. "I'd be obliged if you'd give me some dry clothes to wear," he said.

"Dry clothes?" The round head wobbled on its stalk of a neck. "No, we don't keep any of those, young Will. No need for them."

"Some water then."

The gaunt man shook his head again. "None of that either."

"But when prisoners come—" said Will, his teeth chattering.

"When prisoners come here, they are very quickly executed, young Will," said the man in his scratchy voice. "Or sometimes they just disappear altogether, like they'd never existed at all. Marvellous, isn't it?"

"I'm very cold, Master…"

"Sledd's my name, Master Charles Sledd. But you can call me Charlie. Only if you're telling the truth, mind. I hate it when people call me Charlie then lie to me."

"I won't lie to you, Master Sledd."

"Charlie, boy, Charlie if you're telling me the truth," said Sledd. He resumed his pacing. "So tell me, what sort of a fellow are you?"

"I'm not sure what—"

"I'm asking your means of livelihood, young Will."

Will was so tired and cold he could hardly think. "I'm a glover," he muttered, unsure himself if that was the right answer.

"A what?"

Will suddenly realised that it would be a terrible mistake

230

to offer any trail that might lead back to Stratford and his family. "A player," he said more loudly. "I'm a player, you know, on the stage."

Sledd stopped walking. "A player?" He tutted disapprovingly. "That is very unhappy news. Players are the most excellent of liars, inflaming the people with their falsehoods, steering them into the path of violence."

"It's just stories," Will said, "entertainment."

"That's a very poor excuse for wrongdoing," said Sledd. "But we'll speak no more of it for the present. Now, when you were found floating unnatural in the water—"

"Unnatural?" Will looked up with a glimmer of indignation.

"That's what I was told, young Will." Sledd's voice took on a menacing edge. "And I'll be obliged to you if you don't interrupt me again. Now, when you were found floating in the water, you had a book hidden on your person."

"Yes, that's right."

"And how did it come into your possession?"

"I was delivering it to somebody."

"Somebody? What sort of a name is that – Somebody?"

Will strained to keep his thoughts straight. Walter had made him swear to keep the *Meta Incognita* a secret. "I don't know his name. I had it written down but I lost it."

Sledd locked his fingers together under his chin and

cracked his knuckles. "Well, if you're reluctant to give me a name, I'll have to suppose the book is your own, a book filled with unholy spells and foul enchantments."

"No, they're not spells, Master Sledd," Will protested.

"*Charlie!*" Sledd barked, adding more softly, "if you're telling me the truth."

"I am," Will took a deep breath, "Charlie."

Sledd clenched a bony fist. "That name of mine will burn your tongue if you use it for a lie, young Will, I promise you that."

"I think it's a code. It's written by a philosopher, an astrologer. That's why it's hard to understand."

"A philosopher?" Sledd repeated. "An astrologer? I think what you're trying to tell me is that he's a *warlock*!"

"No, I swear—"

"Swear by what, young Will? By Satan? By Beelzebub? By Asmath and all those other demons you worship?"

"I don't worship any demons!"

"No?" Sledd clamped a claw-like hand on Will's shoulder. "So you're a godly boy then, are you?"

"As godly as any, I hope," said Will, shrinking away.

"The let's pray together," Sledd suggested, releasing his grip. "If you're godly and no witch, you won't choke on an honest prayer, will you?"

Will shook his head. The blood was pounding in his temples and he couldn't stop shuddering.

"That's a good boy," said Sledd soothingly. "Now clasp you hands and bow your head. We'll say a prayer together."

Will locked his fingers and lowered his eyes.

Sledd cleared his throat noisily, then intoned, "*Ave Maria, gratia plena...* "

The prayer was one Will had learned in his childhood. As Sledd's voice tailed off he completed it without even thinking. "*Dominus est tecum...*" *Hail Mary, full of grace, the Lord is with thee...*

Sledd grabbed him by the jaw and forced his head back. Will's eyes snapped open in terror. "Now it's a shame," Sledd declared with a leer, "that a godly boy should come out with a Roman prayer, in Latin and all. It wouldn't trip so easy off the tongue of an honest Englishman."

Will struggled to say something, but he could think of no excuse, no trick. Sledd shoved him clear off the chair and sent him sprawling painfully over the hard, dirty floor. The interrogator's serpent eyes, cold as bullets, fastened on to Will.

"My master, Sir Francis Walsingham, is the Secretary of State," he said. "He has authorised me to do all I deem necessary for the protection of the Queen, this country and the Protestant faith. And here I find you, your heart corrupted by idolatry, leagued with Roman priests and witches to strike down our Good Queen Bess that's been lawfully anointed by God Himself."

Will pushed himself up against the wall and pressed a fist to his mouth to keep silent. Every time he spoke, Sledd found a way to use his words against him. The truth was whatever Sledd wanted it to be and nothing Will said could deflect him.

Sledd stalked him like a predator, looming over him with a contemptuous sneer.

"Give me names, boy," he commanded sternly, "the names of your associates, and maybe God's vengeance will come down more heavily on them than on you."

"I don't know any names," Will sobbed.

"You do," said Sledd, regarding him with pitiless, unblinking eyes, "and by the time I'm done with you you'll beg me to listen to them."

He turned and plucked the lantern from its alcove. "I'll leave you now, young Will, in a darkness of your own making. When I come back I'll have my instruments with me. And what a lively tune I'll play on you then!"

The door clanged shut behind him like the first horrid peal of a funeral bell.

27

Darkness and Light

Will was plunged into a darkness so absolute it snuffed out even the memory of light. His relief at Sledd's departure was quickly eclipsed by a desolate sense of loneliness. He couldn't see his hand in front of his face and had only his aches and bruises to remind him that his body was here at all.

His own breathing sounded strange to his ears, like the sighing of a mournful wind. The only other noises were the marching feet of the guards, the hollow bang of a door or the cries of other souls imprisoned in this fortress.

For the second time that day he was a prisoner, but on this

occasion his situation was infinitely worse. He had no tricks left, no clever ploys. He felt helpless, stupid, worthless.

He crossed his arms over his knees, buried his face in them, and wept.

Should he tell Sledd the truth about Henry Beeston and his players, who were already accused of corruption and sedition? About John Dee, who was rumoured to be a sorcerer? About Grace O'Malley, a wanted pirate? Or about Walter Raleigh, who was involved in a secret plot with the vile Edward de Vere? To speak of them would only make him more guilty, and even worse, it would bring them to Sledd's malevolent attention, dooming them as Will knew himself to be doomed.

None of them knew he was here, and if they did what would they do? Walter and Grace were only concerned with their own schemes and ambitions and now that Will no longer had the *Meta Incognita*, why should they care what happened to him?

That left only God, and with all the trouble that had befallen his father and losing Ann this past winter, Will was sure He had lost any interest in helping the Shakespeares. What did it matter if you prayed before a statue or a bare altar, in English or in Latin, if God didn't listen anyway?

Sobbing, he pressed his wet cheek to the wall. The stone

was as hard and unyielding as fate. And so the night rolled dreadfully by, like a huge granite millstone grinding out the final hours of his life.

With every passing hour Will sank deeper into a well of despair, like a drowning man giving in to the sea. Everything was gone, everything was lost... except for one curious thought jabbing at him like a needle:

There's something in my pocket.

It was such a ludicrous notion to pop up now, he decided he had finally lost his mind. Still, what reason was there for a madman to fight against his delusions? He reached into his pocket and closed his fist around whatever was there. Carefully he brought out his hand and held it directly before his face. Slowly he uncurled his fingers and gasped.

For the barest instant he was sure he saw something there, flickering in the centre of his palm like a tiny star.

Why, it's good luck, Will, he heard his father say. *The prettiest luck in all England.*

At that single moment Will's whole life seemed to hang in the balance, breathlessly suspended between wonder and doubt. It was then the cell door swung open and a wash of light spilled into the room.

Will looked up in astonishment to see a lantern floating

through the air towards him, its flame blazing forth like a jet of living gold. And behind it, their faces illuminated by the glow, came Walter Raleigh and Grace O'Malley.

Will stared at them as though they were a pair of apparitions from the spirit world.

"Is this the prisoner you want, Captain du Champ?" asked a guard from behind them.

Grace thrust herself forward. "Oh yes, that's my sweet boy!" she sniffled, dabbing her eyes with a kerchief. Under her cloak she wore the gown of a fine lady.

"Du Champ?" Will echoed blearily.

"Yes, I've brought your mother here so that she may have a last sight of you before you go to meet your fate," Walter told him gruffly. He was dressed in a soldier's uniform complete with steel helmet.

"Oh, my poor son!" Grace howled, throwing her arms around Will. "How did you come to this?"

She pressed him tightly to her bosom and made a great show of fussing over him. When Will lifted his tearful eyes to meet hers, she gave him a sly wink.

"He was led astray," Walter explained to the guard. "The usual story – bad company, strong drink and women of loose virtue."

"He was never a wicked boy," Grace wailed, "only

lacking in wits, like his father. I warned him he'd come to the gallows in the end."

"Has he been offered any spiritual comfort?" Walter inquired.

The guard looked at him blankly. "Comfort?"

"A Bible, man," Walter snapped impatiently, "and a light to read it by!"

"Those weren't Master Sledd's orders," the soldier answered apologetically.

"Nor did I leave instructions that he should receive visitors!" came Sledd's voice, like iron rasping over stone.

The guard straightened to attention at once. "No, sir, but his mother..." he mumbled as Charles Sledd stepped into the room.

Sledd had a book in his hand and even in his present confused state Will recognised the *Meta Incognita*.

Raleigh set down his lantern and gave Sledd a haughty stare. "And who might you be, sirrah?"

Sledd's lip trembled with outrage. "I am Charles Sledd, the state inquisitor. And you?"

"I am Captain Richard du Champ of the City Guard," said Walter. "I have instructions to deliver this woman into the presence of her son that she might comfort him in his last hours."

Sledd scowled. "I received no notice of—"

"My poor boy!" Grace interrupted shrilly. "What have you done to him?"

"I have treated him as befits a spy and a traitor," Sledd answered stiffly. He tapped the book. "I have evidence of his plotting here."

Walter drew close to Sledd and dropped his voice to a confidential hush. "I see you are a man of discernment and sound reasoning as well as a patriot."

"I am all of those things," Sledd agreed.

"Then you are aware there is a conspiracy afoot and this degenerate youth is merely part of it."

"I had deduced as much from questioning him," said Sledd with a knowing nod.

Walter cast a suspicious glance towards the guard. "We cannot discuss such things in front of minions," he warned in a whisper.

"You, begone and leave us to talk!" Sledd commanded the soldier.

Clearly relieved at being dismissed, the man disappeared up the stairway in a matter of seconds. Sledd probed Walter with his beady eyes. "Now you may tell me all."

Walter took a folded sheet of paper from his pocket and offered it to Sledd. "Here, this letter will explain everything."

Sledd accepted it warily. Opening it out, he read aloud:

> *"Fain would I but I dare not.*
> *I dare, but yet I may not.*
> *I may although I care not*
> *For pleasure when I play not."*

He glanced up sharply at Walter who urged him to continue.

While Sledd read out the rest of the letter with increasing irritation, Grace crept behind him and slipped a stout wooden club out from under her cloak.

> *"I catch, although I hold not.*
> *I burn, although I flame not.*
> *I seem, whenas I would not,*
> *And when I see, I am not."*

Sledd broke off angrily and shook the letter at Walter. "What's this supposed to be? Poetry?"

Grace raised the club and brought it down hard across the back of the inquisitor's head. Sledd dropped to the floor without a word, like a corpse cut from the gallows. Walter knelt down beside him. "Some of my best, actually," he said, retrieving the letter and stuffing it back in his pocket.

As Sledd lay groaning Walter stripped off the inquisitor's own belt and breeches and used them to tie him up. Grace stuffed a gag in his mouth and patted him on the head like a naughty puppy.

Walter opened the door and called out urgently to the guard. He waited till the soldier came rushing into the cell then surprised him with a right hook to the jaw, knocking him into the wall. Before he could recover his senses, Walter and Grace tied and gagged him.

Grace helped Will to his feet. "God's mercy, you're so pale!"

"Can you walk, Will?" Walter asked.

Will nodded.

"We're in a dungeon under the White Tower," said Walter. "It's only a short walk across the courtyard to the Bloody Gate then on to the dock where our boat's waiting."

"We'll be seen," Will objected vaguely.

"Never mind about that," said Grace, hoisting up the hem of her dress. "I've got just what you need right here."

Will made to look away then saw that she was pulling out an extra set of clothes from under the hoops of her skirts. Woman's clothes. Will groaned at the sight of them.

"It's the only way to get you past the guards, Will," said Walter.

Will pulled on the plain dress, straightened the blonde wig and adjusted the padding of his false bosom. "How do I look?"

"You won't be fighting off any admirers," said Walter, "but you'll do."

"Here, keep this in front of your face," said Grace, handing Will her kerchief. "Tears make a wonderful disguise."

Walter picked up the book from where Sledd had dropped it and headed for the stairway. "Now, if we walk briskly but without drawing attention to ourselves," he said, "we might be lucky enough to get clear before anyone raises the alarm. Remember, Will, half your disguise is how you carry yourself."

At the top of the stairs they passed through an arch and out into an open courtyard. The sunlight dazzled Will but he smiled at the blue of the sky as if he were seeing it for the first time.

Keeping close together, they set out towards the gate, trying their best to look as innocent as a family out for a Sunday stroll. At their back loomed the White Tower, the castle that stood in the centre of the grounds. Its white stone bulk dominated the surrounding walls and the score of lesser towers that made up the royal fortress. A flock of ravens burst from the battlements above and filled the air with their horrid cawing.

While striving to keep up with Walter, Will kept his steps small and feminine. He had never expected to be grateful for the hours Tom and Kit made him practice walking like a girl.

They passed only a few people on their way and none paid them any attention. As they approached the gatehouse, however, the officer commanding the guard stepped into their path. He raised a hand and stared curiously at Will.

"Captain du Champ of the City Guard," Walter identified himself. "Open the gate, if you please. I'm late for an appointment with the Lord Mayor."

"I'm sorry to delay you, sir," the officer apologised, "but I don't recall this lady being accompanied by a serving girl when you arrived."

28

Inconstant Allies

There was an awful pause. Then Walter thrust his chest out and fixed the officer with an imperious eye. "So you think a common serving maid is beneath your notice, do you?" he boomed.

The officer was taken aback by the accusation. His mouth opened and closed as he struggled for a reply.

"It's robust young women like this who bear us stout sons to man our walls and crew our ships," Walter declared, slapping Will on the back. He wagged a scornful finger at the officer. "It hardly befits a gentleman to disdain the flower of English womanhood!"

"Yes, sir, of course" the officer stammered humbly. "I didn't mean to—"

"Enough of your yammering, man!" Walter blustered. "Open the gate and be quick about it!"

The officer issued a hasty command to his men who heaved open the gate so fast one of them fell over. They saluted Walter and bowed to the 'ladies' as they passed by.

"That was quite a show, Walter," Grace complimented him under her breath.

"I once had to quell a mutiny at sea with nothing more than iron nerves and a loud voice," said Walter. "Compared to that, hectoring a guardsman is no great feat."

The Tower fortifications were surrounded by a wide moat that had its own dock. Here Lok was waiting for them in a rowing boat, his arms resting on the oars.

Will rubbed his aching head in confusion. "I thought his boat was wrecked."

"We borrowed this one," said Grace with a smirk.

"Yes, and the sooner we get it back where we *borrowed* it from the better," said Walter, unamused.

He cast a backward glance at the gate as they climbed aboard and saw the officer was still watching them. "Best speed, if you please, Lok," he said. "But don't make it look too desperate."

Lok merely grunted and pulled away from the dock. He steered them into a small channel that took them from the moat out into the Thames. As soon as they were lost among the busy river traffic Will gratefully discarded his wig and stripped off the dress.

Sunlight sparkled on the water and a pair of swans drifted by, as graceful as clouds. On one of the passing boats a minstrel was playing a lute while a girl sang along to the melody, a string of happy nonsense words. Will felt a stupid, sleepy smile spread over his face. He was free, free of Sledd, free of the fears that had haunted him through that awful, endless night.

Lulled by the rhythm of the oars, he gave in to his fatigue. His whole body relaxed and he slumped against Grace, who was seated beside him at the back of the boat. She gently wrapped her arm around him and let his head rest on her shoulder. Will's last thought as he drifted off into sleep was that it felt good – very good – to be alive.

When he awoke he was lying on a soft bed with a downy pillow under his cheek. Sitting up with a yawn he stretched his arms and looked around. He was back in the room Walter had rented at the Angel. The afternoon sun was shining through the window and he could hear the buzz of customers in the bar downstairs.

On the table by the bed someone had left apples, cheeses and a half loaf of bread along with a jug of herb-scented water. Will's appetite came roaring back and he set to the meal without pausing for an instant. He couldn't remember anything ever tasting so delicious.

He had munched all three apples down to the core when Walter Raleigh came in. He had exchanged his soldier's jerkin and helmet for a silk doublet and feathered cap so that he looked his usual jaunty self again.

"You're looking much better, Will," he said jovially.

Will gulped down a swallow of water to clear his mouth. "Walter, how did you know to find me at the Tower?" he asked, rounding up the last crumbs of bread and popping them into his mouth.

Walter sat down on the bedside and took off his cap. "Well, once we managed to reach the shore with no sign of you, I asked around among the officers in charge of the raid on the smugglers' ship. Eventually I learned that a boy had been fished out of the river and accused of witchcraft on account of a certain book."

"That book!" Will groaned. "I'll be glad to be rid of it!"

Walter slid a hand under the mattress and pulled out the *Meta Incognita*. "We'll return it to Dr Dee tonight," he said, "as long as we can keep it out of Grace's hands."

"Seeing you and her together like that was the last thing I expected," said Will.

Walter fidgeted uneasily with his sword hilt. "She and I have come to an arrangement." After a pause he said, "I suppose that man Sledd asked you a lot of questions."

"I didn't tell him anything," said Will. "Not about you or Grace or about your scheming with Edward de Vere."

Walter gave him a stern look. "I warned you to forget about that."

Will ignored the rebuke. "I don't know what it is that you're up to, but I think you should know that Mendoza has a hand in it."

Walter laughed. "Now you're letting your imagination run wild. You're still tired, of course."

"I know exactly what I'm talking about," Will insisted, slamming his hand down on his empty plate. "Mendoza told me that England and France would soon be at war."

"I'm sure he and his king would like nothing better," said Walter, "but we're at peace with the French."

"That's not all," Will insisted. "He told Grace and me there were revels taking place at Mortlake tonight. He knew all about it and said that something was going to disrupt them. Something very serious."

"This is all very vague," said Walter.

"No, it's not," said Will, "not if you think about it. The queen's entertaining the Duke of Anjou at Mortlake tonight, isn't she? And he's the king of France's brother."

"It's being kept a secret because of hostility to the proposed marriage between them," said Walter, "but yes, you've guessed right. So where does that lead us?"

"You tell me, Walter," Will countered. "Who are these friends of de Vere's you've been giving information to?"

Walter sighed. "I shouldn't tell you any of this, but I suppose it will all be over in a few hours. They're a group of militant Catholics who want to push the queen into the French marriage. For the sake of secrecy the Queen will have only a minimum escort with her at Mortlake, and they see this as their chance to approach her directly."

"But why are you involved in this?"

"I'm acting on orders from the Secretary of State, Sir Francis Walsingham," Walter replied. "He wants to flush out these conspirators and make an example of them. He'll have men waiting to arrest them when they make their move. I'm sure the Queen is in no danger."

Will thought quickly. "It's not the Queen," he said, "it's the duke. Don't you see? If any harm comes to his brother, wouldn't that force the French king to declare war against England?"

Walter pondered this. "Yes, Mendoza does have agents among our own people. If one of them has infiltrated the plot they might do exactly what you're suggesting."

The door opened and Grace O'Malley strode in. She was still wearing a dress and Will couldn't help noticing how well it fitted her.

"That Mistress Swift of yours keep a grand larder," Grace declared. "I'm ready to fight an army of Spaniards with your Tower guards thrown in for a bit of spice."

"Let's hope it won't come to that," said Walter.

Grace eyed them suspiciously. "What have you two been talking about?"

"We have to go back to Mortlake right away," said Will.

"What's the rush?" asked Grace, brandishing a bottle. "I just bought some wine to celebrate your escape, Will."

"You can stay here and drink all you want, Grace," said Walter, getting off the bed.

Grace set the bottle down and gave Walter a hard look. "You weren't so keen to be rid of me last night after I saved your life, Walter."

"You saved his life?" Will exclaimed.

"When the boat went over he bashed his head off an oar," Grace explained. "He'd have sunk to the bottom if I hadn't caught hold of him and helped him to the shore."

"I already showed you my gratitude," said Walter, not meeting her eye.

"Oh you did that right enough," said Grace with a broad smile.

"And as I promised, I'll see you and your men get safely out of London with no more said about your dealings with Mendoza. But Will and I are heading back to Mortlake. Come on, Will, get your boots on."

Grace spotted the *Meta Incognita* and passed her tongue across her upper lip. "If you're taking that book back to your friend Dr Dee, you'll be wanting me along to help guard it."

"Guard it?" Walter burst out. "You just want another chance to steal it! You're lucky I'm letting you go free."

"Let me go free?" Grace exclaimed. "Walter Raleigh, you couldn't catch me if you had a net as big as China!"

As Will pulled on his boots Grace cast an irritable glance around the room. "Walter, where in damnation's fires did you put my sea clothes?"

Walter pointed to a closet. "They're in there."

Grace yanked open the closet door and peered into the gloomy interior. As she did so, Walter vaulted off the bed and shoved her inside. He slammed the door shut and jammed a table up against it.

"Raleigh, you miserable measle!" Grace cried, beating

her fist on the door. "I'll bury my blade in your backside! I'll string you up by your innards!"

"That's a mean trick, Walter, considering she saved your life," Will said, raising his voice over the tide of obscenities issuing from the closet.

"She'll be a lot safer if she's out of the way," said Walter, grabbing Dee's book, "and so will we. Come on!"

"But we still don't know what the Devil's Fire is," Will reminded him. "Only Grace knows what it means."

"Oh that doesn't mean anything," said Walter dismissively, "but if you want to wait here and ask her about it, you're a braver man than I am."

29

The Stage is Set

"I don't see why we couldn't just ride up to the front door," said Will.

"I told you," said Walter, "this whole thing is a trap. If we go barging in shouting warnings we'll scare off the very men it's designed to catch. And then Walsingham will have my hide for a hearth rug."

Arriving at twilight, they had tethered Walter's horse just outside the grounds of Mortlake. Now they were making their way through Dee's orchard towards the house. The trees were hung with lanterns and coloured ribbons trailed from the branches, catching the light like fiery streamers.

The whole orchard shimmered like a fairy forest and beyond the trees Will could make out the garden where the play was being performed.

The Queen and her entourage were seated with their backs to the house, which was dimly lit as ever in spite of the occasion. Against the dark mass of Mortlake House, Queen Elizabeth was conspicuous as a pillar of snow in her gown of white silk and pearls. She was seated upon a throne of gilded wood while at her side a man in sumptuous blues and greens sat upon a smaller throne. Occasionally he leaned over to whisper a comment in her ear.

"What is it you're going to do if you won't raise the alarm?" Will asked, his nerves jumping.

"I'll have a quiet word with Walsingham," Walter replied calmly, "and he'll ensure the duke is protected."

Burning braziers had been set round the stage area and by their light Will could see the players. There was Henry Beeston as Pluto and Kit as his queen. Ralph was playing Theseus with Tom as Hippolyta . Other members of the troupe were dancing round them, tossing flowers in the air. Will recognised the scene as the wedding of Theseus and Hippolyta, which meant the play was nearly over.

"There's not much time left," he told Raleigh. "If those plotters of yours are going to make their move, it will be soon."

"I see Walsingham there among the royal party," said Walter, "the man dressed in black."

He quickened his pace but was stopped short by three unearthly figures who stepped out of the cover of the trees to bar their way. Their cloaks glistened like fish scales and each one of them had the head of a beast: a fox, a wolf and a crow.

Will was stunned. His first thought was that these must be spirit beings Dee had conjured up as a demonstration of his powers. Then at second glance he saw the animal heads were merely masks and that these were just men in costume.

"They're Walsingham's men," Walter told him, "disguised to look like part of the play."

The three men swept back their cloaks to reveal the swords hanging at their sides.

"Let me pass!" said Walter. "I have to talk to Sir Francis right now!"

The fox raised a hand to stop him. "You'll stay right here. Walsingham will have words with you once this entertainment is over."

"Then it will be too late!" said Will, his voice almost a wail.

Walter clenched his teeth and huffed like a bull shut up in a pen. In a flash he pounced upon the beast men, swinging his fists with the fury of a storm. All three fell back before him, but kept themselves between him and the house.

"Go, Will, go!" Walter yelled, pressing forward his attack.

Will ducked past the crow man as Walter bumped him off balance and raced through the trees. He had to go straight to the queen, no matter what danger that might expose him to. He didn't care about Walsingham's devious plan. He had to save the duke.

The edge of the orchard was close now and he was taking a breath to shout out when he was grabbed by the arm and wrenched to a halt. He spun round, thinking he had been caught by another of Walsingham's guards. His captor, though cloaked and hooded, was someone he recognised at once.

"Grace!" he gasped.

Grace tossed back her hood. "Why so surprised, Will? I've broken out of the deepest dungeons in Ireland. How long did you think a cupboard was going to hold me?"

Will tried to pull away, but she kept a grip on him. "You should have come by river like me," she said. "It's a lot faster. Now just show me where the two books are and I'll let you be," she promised.

"There's no time for all that now!" Will exclaimed. "I have to get to the Queen!"

Grace gave a puzzled frown and he started to slip out of her grasp. Then Will saw it was too late. Four men had emerged from the shadows of the house with stealthy speed and taken up position directly in front of the Queen. Before anyone could make a move to stop them they had drawn swords and formed a cordon around her.

Henry Beeston broke off his climactic speech and joined in the general amazement. A number of men in fairy costumes who had been standing around him now threw back their cloaks to expose their weapons and started forward.

"Back!" one of the conspirators warned. "Give us our say and none need come to grief!"

The Queen sat silently as the duke spoke to her rapidly in French. The conspirators gestured to Walsingham and the other attendants to back away.

"Grace, we have to do something," said Will.

"What are you talking about?" said Grace. "If your English soldiers were worth anything they'd have taken them by now."

Observing where the Queen and Anjou were seated, and remembering how the play was meant to close, Will had a sudden inspiration. "Follow me, Grace!" he said.

He set off towards the area where the play was being

staged, keeping within the tree line. Grace strode along beside him looking baffled and aggravated.

"Where are we going, Will?" she asked. "What in perdition are you up to?"

"One of those men is an assassin," said Will. "He means to kill the Duke of Anjou."

Grace was unimpressed. "And what's that to you or me?"

Will stopped and grabbed her by the edge of her cloak. "If that happens we'll be at war with France and every Catholic in England will be blamed for it. Now will you help me?"

"Oh, Will," Grace moaned, "I'll die a pauper thanks to you. Lead on then!"

As they made their way towards Theseus' wedding party they could hear the lead conspirator making a speech about the ancient ties between France and England, the blessings of marriage and the duties of a sovereign. When he was done, he and his three companions laid their swords down on the grass and knelt before the Queen like obedient subjects.

Will plunged into the bushes behind the marriage pavilion where Theseus was to be wed. Everyone else was too transfixed by the scene before them to pay any attention to what he and Grace were up to.

"It's all over, Will," said Grace. "You're making a great fuss over nothing."

Casting aside their disguises Walsingham's soldiers moved in to arrest the conspirators. Three of them gave themselves up but the fourth suddenly leapt up and drew a pistol. Backing away from the guards he pointed the gun directly at the Duke of Anjou.

"Stay clear," he warned, "or my shot might go astray and hit the Queen."

Queen Elizabeth raised an imperious hand and ordered her men back. Anjou stared aghast at the assassin and gripped the arms of his throne like a drowning man clinging to a piece of driftwood.

"Or maybe you're right after all," Grace said.

Will gazed at the scene and bit his lip. He hoped desperately his plan would work. "Here, look at his," he said, pulling aside some loose bushes to expose John Dee's mechanical scarab.

"God's mercy!" cried Grace, drawing her sword on the monster.

"It's just a piece of machinery," said Will, "a stage prop. But we can use it to save the duke."

Quickly he explained his plan to Grace then crouched down beside the gigantic insect. It was attached to a taut length of rope that ran from this spot in the garden right up to the highest storey of Mortlake House. The Queen's party had been seated directly below this line so they would have a perfect view of the beetle god as it soared overhead, carrying the king and queen of fairies.

The Duke of Anjou was trying very hard to keep his nerve before the Queen. "I do not know what your quarrel is with me, monsieur," he said to the assassin, "but if you would have me ransom my life, I will pay any price you care to name."

"I didn't come here to be bought off with gold," the conspirator answered disdainfully.

The queen rose slowly to her feet and stood as proud and immovable as a statue. Her red hair was like a halo of flame around her pale, painted face.

"I'll thank you to lay down that pistol, sir," she said with cold authority. "This gentleman has done you no harm."

"Great harm has been done," said the assassin. "Our country is sunk deep in heresy and none will make a move to stop it. If the defenders of true faith must be compelled to action, then so be it." His voice grew shrill and brittle as he steeled himself to do the deed.

Will took a hold of the lever that would release the spring mechanism inside the scarab and Grace raised her sword over the rope, gripping the hilt firmly in both hands.

"England is ripe for punishment," the assassin declared,

"so let it come now!" He levelled the pistol directly at Anjou's head. The Frenchman shut his eyes tight and crossed himself.

30

Deus Ex Machina

With a grunt Will jerked back the lever. There was a clank of gears, a rattle of cogs and the scarab lifted off the grass. A gasp went up from the whole crowd as the monstrous creature soared upward into the evening sky, its legs waving, its jaws snapping, its great wings whirring like an angry wind.

The assassin turned to look and his face changed from the crazed ecstasy of a fanatic to an expression of pure terror. The scarab looked like some demonic fiend unleashed by Satan to carry him off into the bowels of Hell.

"Now!" yelled Will.

Grace swung her blade down and sliced straight through the rope in one stroke. The assassin shrieked in horror as the scarab plunged out of the sky towards him. With a sickening crash it smashed him to the ground, crushing him beneath its weight. The wooden framework broke apart under the impact and pieces of machinery spilled out like metal entrails.

The duke jumped from his throne and let out a high pitched giggle of relief. Soldiers rushed forward to drag the assassin, injured but still living, out from under the wreckage of the scarab.

"Will!" Henry Beeston cried out in delight. "Why, you've saved the day, my boy!"

A wave of cheers spread from the players right across the garden to the queen and her courtiers. Ralph, Kit and the others gathered round Will to congratulate him and bombard him with questions.

"There's a name for what you just did," Beeston told him. "On the stage we call it *deus ex machina*, a god from the machine."

"Well, here's an unlooked for sight!" Ralph exclaimed, stepping rapidly away from Grace. He eyed her sword nervously. "You've changed your costume since we last met, Mistress Maddie."

Grace winced at the name. "A lot has changed since then," she said, gazing around. "But where's Walter Raleigh?"

As if in answer to her question, the three guards in their animal masks emerged from the orchard, escorting a disarmed and captive Walter. Dr Dee hailed the men and ordered Walter's immediate release. Slipping away from the players, Grace and Will strode across the garden to join them.

"Well, that was a scene neither you nor Master Beeston could have invented," said Dee. "You played your part particularly well, I thought, Will."

"You built the scarab," said Will. "Without that I don't know what would have happened."

Dee cast a frowning eye upon Grace. "I didn't think you'd be coming back," he said.

"Oh, I'm sure you've missed me something terrible," said Grace with a smirk.

"Don't worry, John," said Walter, clapping Dee on the shoulder, "I've brought your book back." He pulled the *Meta Incognita* from inside his doublet and handed it over.

"Well, that's splendid!" Dee beamed.

The general air of merriment was suddenly shattered by a fearful scream. It was immediately obvious what had caused it. Flames were belching from one of the windows in the west wing. Mortlake House was on fire!

"Is this it, Grace? Will asked. "Is this the fire you warned us about?"

"Yes, but I didn't think he'd really do it!" gasped Grace with a shake of her head.

"Who?" Dee asked her sharply.

"Caleb," she replied. "He told me how he hates you and your books."

"Hates *me*?" said Dee, baffled.

"Yes, he said he'd brewed up something called the Devil's Fire and that it would burn the whole house down."

"Why didn't you tell us all this before," Walter demanded, "instead of leaving us with a damned riddle?"

"If you'll recall, there wasn't much time for conversation!" Grace threw back at him.

"Buckets! Fetch buckets!" yelled Dee, running towards the house. "Bring water from the well, from the river!"

Everyone ran after him to help fight the flames, but Will found himself rooted to the spot. He knew something about this wasn't right. The fire was too small. And why set it in that unimportant part of the house?

"That's not it!" he shouted after the others. "It's just a distraction, a bit of stage business!"

No one paid him any attention, but Will realised now exactly where to find Caleb and the Devil's Fire. He ran to the house and barged through the front door. He was sure there were only minutes left before all would be lost.

31

The Brimstone Circle

The library was as wondrous as ever, the tiers of books rising up like cliffs on every side. But there was something disturbing in the air. Will sniffed and detected the odours of oil, sulphur and other materials from Dr Dee's alchemical laboratory. Up ahead a sickly yellow light flickered over the tops of the shelves.

Will knew time was running out. He turned the last corner and arrived at the centre of the library. There before him was exactly what he had feared.

Working by the light of a dying lantern, Caleb was emptying the last dregs of his chemical brew out of a stone jar. He had spread it in a circle all around him and from this circle further oily trails spread out to every corner of the library.

The brimstone stench was almost unendurable, but Will forced himself to move forward. As soon as he noticed he wasn't alone, Caleb dropped the jar and snatched the lantern up off the table.

"Don't take another step," he warned darkly. "I only have to dash this lamp to the floor and the flames will take us both. You won't be able to escape."

The lantern reflected balefully off the slick, sulphurous liquid and Will saw his toe was almost touching the edge of it.

"I don't believe you want to harm anybody," he said. "That's why you started that small fire first, to make sure the house was evacuated before you set off the real blaze."

"If you stay here you will die," said Caleb. "I spent weeks making my mixture right. At the touch of a flame it will consume this whole house."

"The Devil's Fire," said Will.

"That's what I call it," said Caleb.

The lamplight cast dark shadows over his face, lending him the appearance of a gloating fiend. But Will had seen many times how easily mere appearance could deceive.

"But why?" he asked. "Didn't you say your family used to own this house? Why would you want to destroy it?'"

Caleb bared his teeth in an anguished grimace. "I spoke to the clerk at the church who keeps the parish records," he said. "He told me my family never owned land here, not this house, nothing."

Will felt the pain in his voice. "So it wasn't true," he said. "But that's not the ruin of everything."

"Isn't it? What have I left? I have searched and searched among these books, these cursed books, for the one thing that might still raise me up, the secret of the alchemist's gold, but I couldn't find it. So, since I can't make gold, I learned to make fire instead."

"But there are so many other things to learn," Will pleaded, "better things."

"Do you think I didn't want to learn?" Caleb retorted bitterly. "The Doctor said he would teach me, but he always had something else to do, something more important. For me there was only keeping the house, tending his needs, and what have I to show for that?"

He looked up at the rows and rows of books as if they were a wall imprisoning him. "It's these books he cares about, not me. And when they are gone, he will be nothing, no better than you or me."

Will looked at the wavering flame of the lantern. If Caleb delayed long enough in carrying out his plan, the flame would burn out and he would not have the means to ignite his chemical brew.

"Are you going to kill yourself for something as empty as revenge?" Will asked.

"I belong in the fire. You don't understand, Master Shakeshaft. You don't know what I am." His voice had taken on a sinister edge that made Will's skin crawl

"I've been told from the day I could understand words," Caleb continued in the same unnerving voice. "Children told me first, then their parents. I am the son of a witch, a dabbler in black magic, that's what they said."

"You shouldn't listen," Will began but Caleb shouted him down.

"There is worse! The reason, they said, that I had never seen my father, is that he was the devil. My mother took him as a lover so he would teach her magic." His round, dull eyes stared straight at Will. "Tell me truthfully, would you want to live if that was what you were, if all those voices kept reminding you of it?"

He rubbed a fist against his ear as if the voices he spoke of were taunting him now.

"You have nothing to do with witches or the devil," said

Will. "I've been accused of mixing with both, and it's just something people say out of fear and malice."

"It's what I've been told," Caleb insisted. He glanced anxiously at the lantern. There could be only be another minute or two before the flame died. "Go now, and save yourself! Leave me to the fire."

He raised the lantern up, threatening to dash it to the floor.

Will thought of all the wonders stored in this library, the thousands of volumes. He thought of this great house and the marvellous machines it contained. But most of all he thought of this one wretched soul, so filled with hatred of himself that he was ready to throw away his own life in a futile act of despair.

"I know what it's like to be too afraid to go on living," said Will, "but the darkness will lift, the morning will come. In the end it is better to live."

"For you, perhaps," said Caleb. "Since they call me a devil, I may as well be one." His voice had quieted now. More than anything else he sounded defeated.

Will recalled that only a week ago Caleb had reached out to find some bond of trust between the two of them, even if it was in his own odd way. Will realised he needed that trust now and there was only one way to get it.

He looked down at the stream of sulphurous liquid that lay between them. Its black sheen and stinging stench made him think of the poisonous River Styx the ancient writers said surrounded the land of the dead. Biting his lip to keep his nerve steady, Will stepped inside the brimstone circle and stood at Caleb's side.

Caleb shook his head disbelievingly. "Do you want to die?"

"No, I don't," said Will, "and neither do you. But I have a true story you have to listen to, a story about life."

"It's too late for stories now," Caleb said in a cracked voice. The lantern shook in his hand.

"This is one you've always known," said Will, "but you forgot it. It's about a woman abandoned with her baby son. Though she was alone with no help, she refused to give up. She learned the secrets of plants and herbs, making remedies and cures for the sick. By selling those potions she managed to feed and clothe herself and her child."

He saw Caleb begin to waver, lowering the lantern inch by inch.

"But now that she's gone I have nothing," the sad youth said.

"No, you're wrong there," said Will. "She left you something better than a house or gold – she left you her courage, the courage to go on when everything seems lost.

See." He closed his hand and stretched it out before him. "Just think of it lying in the palm of your hand, and whenever you need it you only have to open your fingers and it's there."

Caleb watched as Will opened his fingers. Then he stared down at his own empty hand, as if something were dimly visible there. Silently he passed the lantern to Will.

As Will grasped the circular handle, the flame flickered out. But they were not in the dark. Another light had appeared. Looking into the white glow they saw John Dee walking towards them, a lamp in his hands. His face looked sad and hopeful at the same time.

"I was listening to what you said, Caleb," he sighed. "I never meant to make you feel that way. When I took you in I meant this to be your home, but I'm an old fool whose mind leaps so quickly from one thing to another that I forget my own good intentions."

Caleb shrank back in confusion. "But I set the fire…"

"It's been put out," Dee assured him, setting his lamp down on the nearest shelf. "And now we must set things right. There is so much I can teach you, but you have to do one thing for me first."

A trace of his habitual suspicion glinted in Caleb's eye. "What?" he asked warily.

"Forgive me," said Dee, extending his hand toward him.

Will watched as Caleb struggled with his conflicting emotions. He rubbed his fingers together nervously then stepped out of the sulphurous circle to shake the doctor's hand. Will followed him, grinning with relief. Only now did he realise that there was sweat running down his back and his heart was pounding.

"Do you think we can get back to the party now?" he asked.

"There would be no party if you hadn't come for me, Master Shakeshaft," Caleb told him.

"Shakeshaft's not my name," said Will. "Somebody just made it up for me. My name's really Will Shakespeare."

"Shake-Spear," Caleb repeated slowly. Will was astonished to see him smile. "That's a hero's name."

"I'm no hero," laughed Will. "I've learned that much. But I'm content to be who I am, and so should you be."

32

The Reign of Mercy

Outside in the garden the saving of the Duke of Anjou and the dousing of the fire provided a double reason for celebration. Kemp and Ralph struck up a jig on the lute and drum and the Queen's maids danced upon the lawn with any gentlemen who could push their way ahead of their rivals. Spices were tossed on to the burning braziers to produce a festive scent so that the air was filled with music and sweet fire. Extra barrels of beer and wine were brought up from the village tavern and it looked to Will like the party would go on all night.

He was sharing a beer with Walter and Grace when the

Queen approached them with her diminutive attendant Madame Thomasina at her side. In her white gown with its gleaming pearls and her pale makeup she might have been a ghost or an angel descending to earth from a higher realm. Will gulped as they all bowed low, not knowing whether she had come to commend or condemn them.

"Dr Dee has been explaining to me his plans for the further exploration of the Americas," Queen Elizabeth said to Walter. "He says you are the man to lead our next expedition there."

"I would be honoured to serve Your Majesty in that capacity, and to claim those lands in your name," Walter answered humbly. He bowed again, so low Will was afraid he would fall on his face.

"And you two," said the Queen, "Mistress O'Malley and Master Shake-Spear, I believe I have you to thank for saving the life of my good friend the Duke of Anjou."

Will tried to say something courtly as Walter had done, but all that came out was, "Yes... I... we... many thanks, Your Majesty."

Grace did not appear in the least overawed. "Oh, we had a spot of luck, that's all," she said.

"Never the less," said the Queen, "your performance was far superior to that of the duke himself."

Will dared not look closely enough to be sure, but he thought she was smiling.

A man clad in pitch black robes with a large collar of white lace appeared at the Queen's side. Will realised this must be her Secretary of State, Sir Francis Walsingham, whose name he had heard more than once these past few days.

"Your Majesty, the assassin will not live to see morning," Walsingham reported. "His wounds are too severe."

Queen Elizabeth nodded. "See he's made comfortable and send to the church for someone to tend his soul."

"I'll have the others sent to the Tower to await execution," said Walsingham.

"No, Sir Francis," said the Queen. "Confiscate their property and banish them, but let them keep their lives."

Walsingham looked aghast. "They drew swords in your presence! You must make an example."

"Of what?" the Queen retorted. "Cruelty? We have been spared a ruinous war. Let us be sparing in our punishments."

Walsingham averted his shrewd, intelligent eyes and bowed his head in acquiescence.

"I believe this lady requires transport back to Ireland," the Queen told him. "Please arrange it."

Walsingham looked up sharply. "Your Majesty, this is

Grace O'Malley the notorious pirate. For years she has preyed upon—"

"No doubt she has," said the Queen, cutting him off with a regal wave of her hand. "My only concern is the service she has done me."

"But that does not absolve her of her many crimes," Walsingham insisted.

"Today it does, Sir Francis," said the Queen in a tone that made her secretary quail. "If a queen is to rule justly she must also rule with mercy."

"I'm very happy to accept your help, Your Majesty, but this business of saving England is going to ruin my reputation," Grace joked.

"I think," said the Queen with a smile, "that the sooner we get you out of England the better it will be for both of our reputations. But in the meantime we can share a cup of wine together. I'm sure we'll find something to talk about."

"Oh, Your Majesty, there are such tales I could tell you, to be sure!" Grace laughed. As she walked off with the Queen she looked back and said, "I'll save you a dance, Walter – if you can catch me."

Alone with Walter and Will, Walsingham shook his head disapprovingly as his sovereign carried on an animated conversation with the pirate queen. His brows narrowed as he turned to Walter. "That was a dangerous turn of events. If Mendoza was involved as you say, I shall have to keep a close eye on him."

Will thought of the trouble that would have befallen his family and friends if they hadn't been able to stop the would-be killer. "You would have done better to leave things alone instead of luring those men on," he told the two of them.

"You are only a boy," said Walsingham coldly, "with no understanding of such matters. It was necessary to expose them before they attempted some worse treason."

"But that's not all, is it?" said Will. "You wanted them to confront the queen."

"You're right, Will," said Walter. Walsingham tried to silence him with a warning look, but he carried on. "It's the Queen's nature to rebel against anything someone tries to force on her. She'll never marry the Duke of Anjou now."

"You must understand the importance of this, Master Shakespeare, and why you must never speak of it," said Walsingham sternly. "From now the Queen will remain single and childless, but because of that England will stand upon her own two feet, relying on no other nation for her protection. That is the destiny of your country."

"So you've been deceiving everyone," said Will, "the Queen as much as the conspirators."

"It's a shady business, Will," said Walter, "I don't deny that, but you have to believe we acted in the best interests of England."

"I'm sure you believe that's what you're doing," said Will.

Walsingham stared at the two of them long enough to satisfy himself that his secret would remain safe. "I must go now," he said, "and prepare some documents for the Queen to sign."

"What sort of documents?" Will asked suspiciously. "Are you going to arrest even more people?"

"Not at all, Master Shakespeare," Walsingham replied evenly. "They will authorise the construction of ships, a great navy to defend England against any possible attack and to carry our explorers to the farthest corners of the earth. As I told you, it is a matter of destiny."

He made to leave, then stopped. "But speaking of arrests," he said, "I have received a report of an escape from the Tower. A young man named *Will* curiously enough."

"I... I don't know anything about it," said Will unconvincingly. The memory of that terrible night at the tower came rushing back on him like an huge black wave.

"You can't mean to punish the boy after all he's done for us!" said Walter vehemently.

Walsingham quirked an eyebrow. "Well, the law is the

law, but as you say, he has been of some use. Master Shakespeare, I will see you are provided with a royal pardon, absolving you of any wrongdoing you have been guilty of up to this time."

"Thank you!" exclaimed Will, unable to contain his relief. "That's very good of you."

Walsingham made a sour face as he turned away. "If the Queen insists on being merciful then so, I suppose, must I."

Mortlake, XXIInd Daye of August, 1579

My Dearest Parents,

I am very happy to bring you the glad tidings that I am alive.

I am back at Mortlake House enjoying the hospitality of Dr Dee without the burden of editing his playe. Lord Strange's Men have moved on and I believe Master Henry Beeston is attempting to negotiate a season for them at the Curtain Playhouse in London. I have shared many happy times with the Players and though I am sad to see them go, I am haunted by the certainty that we will meet again.

Master Henry Beeston sayes the whole Worlde is a stage and over Time a man must playe many parts. I feel I have played a sufficient variety of parts these past weekes to last me a considerable time. But who can tell? Perhaps my greatest role still awaits me.

I have - through a turn of events you will find it difficult to credit - obtained a document which will allow me to walk right up to Sir Thomas Lucy's front door and thumb my nose in his face. With this protection I intend to return to Stratford in the company of a merchant caravan departing London in four dayes time.

In the meanwhile I am exploring the wonders of Dr Dee's library. What a wealth of stories there are here translated from the Italian, French and Spanish! Knights, fair maidens, rescues and miracles! I will strive to remember as many as I can and relate them to you upon my return.

I will be bringing with me a gift from Dr Dee - the entire manuscript of Pluto and Proserpina. I hope we have a cupboard dark enough - and large enough! - to hide it in. He sayes he has not the time to bring it to completion, but that if I should ever incline to a literary career, I maye treat it as my own.

Caleb, the unhappy fellow I have told you of, is much changed of late. I see him now working alongside the Doctor, studying works of Medicine and preparing curative potions. His face is more open, his posture more confident, and I swear I hear him laugh now at least twice a daye. It is as if a life-sapping poison has been drained from his soul and a healthier nature is asserting itself, like a Rose bursting free of the frozen Earth.

I too am much changed, though I hope you will recognise me still. The gifts you gave me when I left Stratford have served me well and helped me win through many adventures, none of which I feel it is prudent to commit to paper and ink. Suffice it to saye I have learned much of my own nature and of the world about me that I was ignorant of before.

It has been a tale of trials and perils that I feared might prove my undoing, but I have survived them all. And so, as Walter once said to me,

All's Well That Ends Well.

Your devoted Sonne

Will Shakespeare

Afterword

Almost all of the stories in Shakespeare's plays are taken from books he had read. The main exceptions are *A Midsummer Night's Dream* and *The Tempest*, for which no direct sources have been found. The wizard Prospero in *The Tempest* is widely believed to be inspired by the court astrologer Dr John Dee and many scholars believe that *A Midsummer Night's Dream* was created as an entertainment for Queen Elizabeth I.

This led me to suppose that perhaps the germs of these plays were to be found in some events of Will's early life of which history has left no trace, and so this tale was born. The historical roots of the story are as follows.

In 1579 the Duke of Anjou arrived secretly in England to persuade Queen Elizabeth to marry him. Elizabeth's court was divided between those who were for and against the marriage, but the most powerful voice was that of her Secretary of State, Sir Francis Walsingham, a Puritan who vehemently opposed England entering into such a union with a Catholic country. We learn from John Dee's own diaries that he was one of the few people who knew of Anjou's arrival.

Recent biographers of Walter Raleigh believe he was acting as an agent of Walsingham at this time in order to expose members of a Catholic conspiracy. He was also a friend of John Dee and the two frequently discussed matters of navigation and the exploration of the New World.

To the explorers of the Elizabethan age, the Northwest Passage was a geographical Holy Grail, holding out a promise of immense wealth, but all their attempts to find it failed. The legend of the Passage continued to lure explorers into the Arctic seas for another four centuries until the route was finally discovered by the Norwegian Roald Amundsen in 1903.

All the major characters in the story are based upon real

people, including Grace O'Malley the pirate queen, Lok the Inuit boatman, and the inquisitor Charles Sledd.

I should explain that some of the more fantastic parts of the story are also grounded in fact. While he was a student at Cambridge John Dee built a huge mechanical scarab, just like the one I describe, as a prop for a production of Aristophanes' play *The Peace*.

We have no evidence that Grace O'Malley was in London in 1579, but she did arrive there some years later and met with Queen Elizabeth. After what must have been an interesting conversation, Elizabeth gave the pirate queen full permission to carry on with her warlike activities. I have simply moved their meeting forward in time.

Finally, could Will really have escaped from a secure fortress like the Tower of London by disguising himself as a girl? Well, in 1716 the Earl of Nithsdale was imprisoned in the Tower after a failed Jacobite uprising in Scotland. He escaped with the help of his wife, who disguised him as a woman.

For more information about *Will Shakespeare And The Pirate's Fire* please visit my website at

www.harris-authors.com